A JOURNEY INTO ROMANCE

J N Banerjee

MINERVA PRESS
NEW DELHI
MIAMI LONDON SYDNEY

A JOURNEY INTO ROMANCE

ISBN 81 7662 026 2

First Published 2000 by
MINERVA PRESS
13 Palam Marg
Vasant Vihar
New Delhi – 110 057

Printed & bound in India
For Minerva Press (India) Pvt. Ltd.

A JOURNEY INTO ROMANCE

To Bulu
With love

A good traveller is one who does not know where he is going. A perfect traveller does not know where he has come from

J N Banerjee

CONTENTS

ONE

Since my childhood I have had an insatiable fascination for historical places – and still have. So much so, that whenever opportunity beckons, I set out to visit them. But ever since I had settled down in Delhi, India's traditional capital, this had become my pet obsession.

Early one October morning, last year, after attending the first ever All-India Young Creative Writers' Meet at Bangalore, I arrived at Pune, enroute to Mandu.

Snatching a few brief hours, of a short stopover, I hailed a cab on the street and headed straight for The National Defence Academy, Khadakwasla, to have a glimpse at one of the most successful projects of our first Five-Year Plan. My arrival, after a light shower on the way, was greeted by a burst of sunshine and I took this, for a good omen.

Depositing me at the 'Pashan Gate' of the Academy, the taxi disappeared fast down the sloping hill road, towards Chatursbringi. Holding the all-important attaché case, I straightened my back for a moment and stood, kissed by the fresh morning wind.

The National Defence Academy, a vivid example of modern architecture where the past and the present mingle freely, lay sprawling on the Rajwade plains, before me. The main street, which bisected the Academy, ran on a north-south axis. The college, a red-stone building with a dome, stood in the heart of this military town. Cadet campuses and the Mess, the science block with its electrical and mechanical wings, the cinema, the parade ground, stadium, gymnasium, playground, swimming pool built harmoniously amid the low hills, where peace and quiet were abidingly present.

I covered the whole area on foot, imprinting their architectural splendour in my mind. After this sweet fulfilment, I stopped to light a cigarette. A short thirty second later, as I resumed my walk, a flight of wild ducks flew overhead, screaming, their shrill caused by the sound of gunfire.

From the hilltop village, bullock carts, festooned with mango leaves, rattled by, carrying temple-going female folk, dressed in their customary nine-yard *saris* and beautiful nose rings. The lap-held trays and baskets, laden with flowers poised for offering to the God, merged in harmony with their faith and belief. The best-liked *gajras* made of *mogra* flowers, aristocrat among jasmines, were looped in single strands like carved ivory, suspended from their plaits, added serenity to the attire. Singing hymns and clapping hands to the rhythm of the tune as they went past me, the *gajras* swayed, keeping pace with the swaying heads.

I had known all along that Maharashtrians, specially the women, have a good eye for flowers. They find a use for them almost everywhere and everytime – from birth to death, arrival to departure and from home to temple.

Enchanting marigold flower garlands adorned the bullocks their horns, too, were decorated with tiny flower circlets. The carts drifted away languidly, leaving a spicy fragrance behind. Semi-charmed, I shouted at those village beauties, 'How far is the temple?' No one answered. A villager looked at me, as if I were an alien. I asked him meekly, 'Do you mind if I join you?' Shrugging indifferently, he hurried off, down the hill road. Non plussed, I looked on, with my eyes fixed on the disappearing figure. About this time, fresh air from the sunny hillside came blowing into my face, healing my hurt feelings.

The twisting road, now empty and silent, gently sloping down, made a sharp U-turn, almost touching the lake. There I stood for a minute, looking at the black-green water, gilded by sunlight. A little distance away, a small hut, shaded by a giant banyan tree, stood nonchalantly. A large signpost, reading PEACOCK BAY, which carried a picture of a peacock, along with the plea 'Don't Disturb Our National Bird', was prominently nailed to the tree's huge trunk, about ten feet above the ground.

Despite the long walk and aching legs, I searched all around for one, but nothing, not even a feather, lay anywhere. At that instant the forlorn cry of a peacock, from the grass-covered hills, pierced the stillness, amply compensating my disappointment.

Peacock Bay, the finest spot in Khadakwasla, is aptly named. My eyes, filled with the scenic magnificence of the place, suddenly fell on an oncoming taxi. About a hundred yards away, as the taxi drew up, out came a modern looking girl and a boy, who walked quickly towards the lake, borne along by their excitement for each other.

The sight of a taxi in such a remote spot was a pleasant surprise. After turning round, when it came crawling towards me, I whooped with joy. Pulling up within a yards of where I was standing, the taxi driver smiled at me, opening the passenger door, which added to my delight.

'Thanks for stopping.' I expressed my gratitude and hopped in.

The clock on the dashboard showed eleven. I glanced at my watch; it also showed eleven. Then, from a school close by, the clock chimed eleven. The last whirr and clang were just over, when, magically, all the clocks in the world harried their clanging down my ears, as if to say: *Sanchu, you've got to reach Pune by twelve.*

'Hurry, driver. I don't have much time.'

Nodding politely to my mumbling, the driver turned the ignition keys and the engine coughed to life. Just as he was about to put the taxi into gear, I heard an, 'Excuse me', which sounded like a plea for help. Turning, I found, bending close to the window on the other side, a teenaged girl, with a striking face, suitcase in hand and a travel-bag slung from her shoulder, craning her neck inside. The questioning look in my eyes prompted her to ask, 'Are you going to Pune?'

I, about to say, 'Yes', changed my mind and simply humoured her with, 'Where else does this road go, Miss?'

The next moment she realised her mistake and the very thought of it, pushed her into a fumbling confusion. To get over the mistake she stammered, 'I...I...I mean Pune Railway Station.'

Giving no answer to this, I regarded her, feeling a little curious, a little puzzled.

That face! Unbelievably beautiful!

Beautiful, not in an ordinary way, but in the way a work of art is beautiful. The serenity of a Maharashtrian face and the quiet refinement of a Bengali, seldom unify in one face and I wondered how this strange girl had acquired this rare combination.

The moment she became aware of my scrutiny, blood rushed to her face. She stirred, pursed her lips and the words, which had been clogged on the tip of her tongue now, tumbled out.

'It's nearly an hour since I've been standing in this godforsaken place, but there is no bus,' she moaned. And, quickly managing a wan smile, added, 'Carrying a few things for a sick friend I'm visiting in the Sassoon Hospital.'

Not convinced by her tale of woe, I asked, 'So now?'

'Well,' she replied, breaking into a hesitant smile, 'I was hoping you would let me share your cab.'

'You're very imaginative.'

Evidently, my tepid response blocked the girl's advances, yet she pretended that her ears had deceived her. She waited, clutching at the hope that she would be invited, but I didn't. Taking my silence as refusal, she stepped backwards.

Once again, reflecting upon the situation, I had a sudden insight as to what was right. And when I asked 'Don't you want to come?' her disappointment passed quickly. Leaping, she came back.

'Yes, awfully much!'

'Do come.' I opened the taxi door for the damsel in distress.

'I'll pay half the fare if you…'

'Oh, now' – I cut her short – 'don't talk about payment. It'll be my pleasure.'

Without any further ado, she heaved onto the empty seat and sat by my side, pleased and happy. Impeccably dressed, perfectly proportioned body, glossy black hair, dark eyes, rosy cheeks, mysterious. When I was filling myself with her beauty, futilely trying to find some imperfection, the taxi shot forward.

Two

The rainy season was over and the hills of the Western Ghats were a riot of lush green. Leaning out of the window, the strange girl was crooning a racy pop tune to herself while, in silence, I was watching the stray clouds scudding across the sky until my suspicion got the better of me. Lest she doubted my intention, I crafted a question as tactfully as I could:

'Hope you aren't running away.'

She put on her sunglasses before answering. 'No indeed,' and she repeated her earlier statement, 'Carrying a few things for a sick friend I'm visiting, in the Sassoon Hospital' making it impossible to probe any further. But her intonation suggested that she was hiding the truth. With this in mind, I shifted my gaze from her to the passing, mountainous scenery.

Overhills and valleys, through peaceful villages monotonously similar, made of grey, mud-stone huts, the taxi purred, never having to sound the horn.

From Hingne, the road wound among the low hills for about five miles and then, in a series of graceful curves, among cashew and guava gardens, descended towards Pune, once the proud capital of the Maratha Empire and now, one of the finest centres of learning.

The mystery girl glanced through her sunglasses with uncertainty and her mind seemed to be in a catacomb of doubt and fear. But when the taxi passed the Deccan Gymkhana, she let out a breath, which she had imprisoned far too long.

As the taxi rolled past the *Junglee Maharaja Temple*, I told the driver to stop at the Sassoon Hospital.

Not long after, the taxi screeched to a halt, outside the wrought iron gate of Pune's oldest house of suffering and hope: SASSOON HOSPITAL.

Nearly a minute passed, yet my companion did not move.

'Sassoon Hospital,' I said, holding the taxi door slightly open.

She showed no inclination to move, let alone get off.

'Sassoon Hospital,' I repeated sharply. But she remained motionless as before.

My irritation increased. Then, in a sudden impulse I muttered an obscenity aiming, at her, but that, too, was lost. She seemed so self-absorbed, so distant. For another tedious minute, I watched her silently, mulling over this unpleasant situation. Finally, I shouted:

'Your Sassoon Hospital, Miss.'

'Sassoon Hospital?' She asked, shaken out of her reverie.

'Your sick friend must be eagerly expecting you.'

'My sick friend?' She was all at sea. 'Who?'

'You didn't tell me the name. Did you?'

'Didn't I?' Her angelic face expressed innocent surprise. Somewhat charmed by her innocence, I was wondering what I had let myself into. Suddenly, an idea struck me. I fished out a hundred rupee note from my wallet and offered it to her, by way of inducement.

'Buy some flowers and fruits for your sick friend.'

She drew back nervously, 'Oh no, no.'

'Please take it. After all, you've come all the way to visit your sick friend. To carry some flowers and fruits would be more natural than meeting her empty-handed.'

She squirmed, 'I don't need any money.' Don't feel shy about it. I am not offering it to you. It's for your sick friend.'

She, by then, had got over her initial embarrassment.

'To tell you the honest truth, I don't have any sick friend in the hospital.'

'Good heavens, you lied?'

'Yes. I lied,' came the unhesitating reply.

'But why?'

'I don't know why.'

'Perhaps, to fool me?' This time my voice was tight.

'Oh no. Why should I?' There was a puzzled expression in her eyes.

A brief silence.

In that brief silence I studied her face.

There was character and strength in that pretty face, as well as determination in the dark eyes and a touch of obstinacy in the resolute chin. Aggressive, yet vulnerable.

'Where do you intend to go?' I felt impelled to ask.

'I wish I knew,' she smiled ruefully, 'but I haven't the slightest idea.'

'How very strange!'

To my muttering, she replied instantly, 'I'm afraid I'm giving you an awful lot of trouble.'

'Think nothing of it. Please tell me if I can help you in any way.'

'Thanks for being so nice,' she said, without any trace of awkwardness. 'Hope you don't mind my coming with you to the station.'

'Not at all.' Then, turning to the driver, I said, 'Pune Station.'

As the taxi continued its remaining ten-minute run, the seasoned urbanite from within, began warning me to leave her at the station and break this unnecessary tie up, once and for all.

At a slack moment, she clutched my arm.

'Yes?'

'Would you have any objection to taking me as your travelling companion?' Her voice was firm, her eyes entreating and her grip tightening.

The girl's request was very romantic but much too sudden for me. Pretending not to have heard her, I asked:

'What did you say?'

She said it again, unhesitatingly and in the same breath, she asked, 'Do you suspect me to be a "boy-trap"?'

'No. If I did, I'd never have given you a lift.'

'That means I can come with you.'

'No.'

'But I have decided to come with you.'

'But I have decided not to take you with me,' I said, solemnly trying to imitate the girl's locution.

'Shouldn't you tell me the reason?'

'See, you hardly know me, or I, you.'

'Do you believe in instinct?'

'To a point, yes.'

'My instinct tells me I can trust you.'

'But instincts can be wrong.'

'May be with others. More often than not, my instincts have been right.'

I was mum, not knowing what to say. A silent war was going on within me – Would I be right, or wrong, in giving her the lift?

She was saying, 'You don't think I am a boy-trap; you don't mind giving me a lift; you believe in instinct and yet, you don't want me to come with you. May I know why?'

'Because you're a lovely young girl.'

'Does it make so much of a difference to you? My being a lovely young girl?'

'Yes, it makes all the difference in the world.'

'I don't understand...'

'Whether you understand or not, I can't take that risk.'

She did not believe me. She looked at me with an expression that clearly said, she was not convinced. She thought I was putting on an act. Boys do this sort of thing, for a good impression. In a final effort she asked:

'You really don't want me to come?'

'Sorry, Miss. Extremely sorry. I cannot afford to travel, taking a golden Venus along with me.'

'If that's all that is worrying you, have no fears about me. I assure you, I'll not use my beauty as a weapon.'

'Still, it can cause trouble. There are instances...' She clapped a hand over my mouth as I tried to cite a hearsay case, from memory.

'I suppose now you're going to quote a few historical facts for authenticity. That's unnecessary. I've read them all and I think they're all exaggerations.'

'Miss, please note, in refusing to take you with me, I needn't quote any historical fact, nor do I have to take recourse to acting. Understand?'

'Goodness me, when did I say that?'

'Denial is easier than admission.'

'If I have really said anything like that, I must have said it without thinking.' She smiled, but seemed a bit nervous.

Heard her? Not a word of regret. This elegant audacity was her natural self. Anyway, I was more or less firm, that after reaching Pune Station we would go our separate ways. So, just for fun, returning to the topic, I said, 'In such cases, the public always holds the man responsible if anything goes wrong.'

'But why should anything go wrong when you're with me?' She flattered me, feeling confident that I would change my mind. When I did not say anything, she changed her tune. 'Please let me come with you. I wouldn't be of any trouble really, and...'

'I'm sorry, Miss.' It was time to be tougher and less emotional.

'But you're not being fair,' the inveterate arguer said bitterly. 'You shouldn't hold my beauty against me.'

'Thereby, I avoid complications.'

When she spoke after a moment's silence, her voice was strangely tinged with annoyance.

'What kind of a man are you? At first sight I took you to be the finest gentleman. I never thought you'd be unjust.'

'Thank you for voting me as the finest gentleman, but it doesn't alter my decision.'

Failing to force the decision in her favour, she muttered, 'If I were you, I'd never refuse.'

'But you're not I', I said, cutting the topic off.

In the silence that followed I found her eyes studying me intently.

'The best thing for you to do', I suggested, 'is to go back to where you belong.'

She showed no disappointment, but her brows furrowed.

'Is that final?' She asked in a steady voice.

'Yes, that is if you are not running away.'

'Don't you see?' She burst out, 'I had to do it. Playing with children...singing with children...eating with children...sleeping with children...I'm fed up! Absolutely fed up!'

Intrigued, I echoed her words, 'Playing with children...singing with children...eating with children...sleeping with children...'

'Dear me, you don't understand. I'm not talking about home but the school hostel. I'm a teacher.'

'Good God! You are a schoolteacher!'

'Yes, I was', she said composedly, correcting the tense.

'You don't look like someone who could have ever loved blackboards, textbooks or lesson plans.'

'You can believe me, because, you see, I always tell the truth.'

'Always?'

'But of course!'

'Except your Sassoon Hospital prank.'

'Oh, that was', she said with a smiling frankness, 'an excuse for the lift.' As I shot her a quick, frowning glance, she added virtuously, 'Believe me, I'm not a liar.'

'All right, Miss, I'll take your word for it.' Then, watching her carefully for an instant, I asked. 'How long had you been teaching?'

'Three months.'

'And, in three, short months, you're fed up?'

'You think three months are not enough?'

'Well, they may be with those modern freaks, who always have to test themselves, stretch their wings and try new winds.'

'Oh, it's a tiring job. Besides, the valley holds nothing for me. I have my future to think about. I shall never go back. Never-never-never-never-never!'

'Why lament? That doesn't make much sense.'

My cool rejoinder calmed her down. She numbly stared at my face and mumbled, 'I'm sorry.'

We could see the Pune Railway Station quite clearly now.

'What time is our train?' She asked in the plural.

'Well,' I glanced at my wristwatch and replied in the singular, stressing the pronoun, 'my train leaves at 12.30.'

She almost shuddered at *my*, she had a lurking fear that I would abandon her. She took a deep breath and composed herself.

'Why do you say *my* train? Are you not taking me along?'

'Are you not afraid, Miss? You hardly know me.'

'How surprising! After travelling twenty-five kilometres together, you say this.'

'But that's not enough to know a stranger.'

'Stranger we were, when we first met. Not anymore.'

'I'm not as sure as you are, though I wish I were.'

'You're fooling yourself. The sooner we dump the 'stranger' bit, the better for us.'

'Look, being a peace loving man, I prefer to be a bit careful, rather than run into a mess.'

'What makes you so, mess-prone?'

'The trouble with you girls is, that you get all excited about nothing; and then...'

'Why panic? You'll not land in any trouble.'

'Thank you. I feel reassured.'

Her face spread into a mystique smile, a smile that only a woman could have.

Three

In front of the station, as the taxi stopped, the girl picked up her things from the front seat, quietly stepped out on to the step and waited.

After paying off the cabby when I got out, she said:

'The offer stands – my sincere companionship.'

She was a woman and she was giving me a choice.

'I'm honoured,' I told her. 'But I don't want to commit the biggest blunder of my life by accepting your tempting offer.'

'If those are your parting words, then why in the world did we meet?' She smiled enigmatically, giving me the full treatment with her great, dark eyes.

The message, plain enough though, was very touching.

'This world is full of willing people. Why does it have to be me?'

The question jolted the girl, but her nature demanded she make a last attempt.

' Make up your mind. A cultured and refined companionship is not easily found.'

Doubts still lingered, judging by the look in her eyes, but there was confidence in her voice.

Was she bitten by the travel bug, the lure of adventure and all that? Or was it a case of a schoolgirl, suddenly finding herself out of the convent, with the world at her feet? Assailed by doubts, I looked intently into her blameless, innocent face.

Without flinching, she asked again, 'Yes, or no?'

The steel will behind the innocence overpowered me and, consequently, I gave in, thus once again proving my inability to get rid of her.

'Okay. Please collect my luggage from the left luggage hall and wait for me at the entrance. I'll only be a minute.' Handing her the luggage receipt, I ran for the ticket counter.

Unable to get two second class berths, I felt disappointed. The kind, booking clerk offered me a second class coupe for two people, as an alternative. This was available against cancellation. And I accepted it without a thought.

When I rejoined her, I found her waiting at the main entrance with the luggage on the porter's head.

'You're very kind,' she said with a charming smile on her face, as we entered the platform.

'Always. Especially to young ladies.

'Oh, really?'

'Honestly.'

After happily settling down in the coupe, I noticed that my travelling companion, visibly perturbed, was gazing out, with unseeing eyes.

The coupe for two people must have frightened her into thinking that something horrible was going to happen as soon as the train started.

'Afraid?' I asked her casually.

'Of what?' She countered, not even turning her head.

'If you're feeling unsafe, kindly get down before the train starts.' I gave her the option.

For about ten seconds she regarded me critically, then said, 'I don't think this coupe is unsafe...All the same, thank you for the option.'

By this time, I had realised that she wasn't from the boy-trapping stock. Rather, she was a discontented teenager, ridding herself of the shackles of parental authority and embarking upon the unknown and unrestricted world. Besides, she became unusually interesting. Her quietness provided me with the opening I needed.

'I think it would be in the fitness of things, if you told me something more about yourself.'

She turned to me with a slight start. First, her eyes took a cool look at me, then she manufactured a Mona Lisa smile.

'In this lousy world of ours, where nobody cares for anybody, how come you care so much for me?'

'Think I'm slightly old-fashioned.'

'There's no need to think. You're just what you said.'

The unexpected backfire, literally hit me across the face. While I was still nursing the wound she went right on, driving her point home. 'But before I fill your ears with my biography, let me know if you have already formed any nasty idea about me.'

I bristled for a moment, as one does, when put on the defensive.

'No. It never entered my mind,' I assured her, in an honest voice. 'But why do you ask?'

'Because most men hardly bother about a woman's dignity.'

'It seems you know a lot about men.' My tone made it plain that her remark was not appreciated.

'Yeah.' She jeered at me with a smile. Then, she startled me by saying, 'Please don't mistake me for a modern *Seeta* or a sophisticated *Draupadi.* Besides, I cannot concoct pleasant Cinderella stories about myself to entertain you.' She paused. It was only after I had swallowed this heavy quinine dose that she ranted on, 'But before you let the wings of your obscene imagination fly, let me enlighten you. Even by mistake, let us not treat each other with, that old-fashioned commonly called emotion, love. We have been doing that, for centuries and there is no purpose in repeating it. In other words, no falling in love and no monkey business. You'll have to accept that. Understand?' Eventually, the finicky girl wound up the ultimatum, in the most scathing tone that teenagers specially reserve, for roadside Romeos.

Her adolescent pride, her random way of speaking without any fear of consequences, amazed me. Yet, I managed to conceal my amazement and remained the attentive listener, as she poured out about herself.

'I'm not a sweet sixteen. I'm nineteen. A Harvard graduate. Majored in English Literature, though not academically very brilliant. I know dancing and I'm not a bad singer. I paint and drive well and there is nothing I don't know about care. I was never short of admirers. But none was ever allowed to get too close to me.' A truculent, threatening note, had crept into her voice, with the last two words.

How unfortunate! I can't even make a single claim, compared to her five diverse credits. Filled with a sense of inferiority, while I was cursing myself, she was exulting in her fancied superiority.

I am unable to say why I was tolerating her boastings. May be because I was hooked by her looks, which appeared both demure and provocative, an irresistible combination.

Suddenly, there was a rude jerk. I listened to the train being coupled to an engine. And, as the train pulled out of the station, I opened the interrogation once again.

'Why did you take up a profession that you couldn't stick to?'

'You may call it a fancy.'

'Fancy? To leave home for a petty, teaching job can never be a fancy,' I interposed.

Let me mention that there was something about her, that made one certain she didn't need a petty, teaching job.

'Does that sound too absurd?'

'It does.'

'All right. Then don't call it a fancy – call it madness.'

'But you aren't mad.'

'I'm not. But you will make me mad.'

'What do you mean? Shouldn't I ask anything about you?'

'Do ask. But don't ask me anything personal.'

'Miss, you must agree, as companions, we must know each other a little more than strangers.'

'Have I said, no?'

'But you haven't told me yet, why you left home.'

'I hadn't just left home, I had escaped.'

'Escaped what?'

'Marriage.'

'How could you have been such a fool, to have chucked away marriage? You know, women, over the centuries, consider marriage as a passport to a new life. Besides, being smart, modern and articulate, you could be a valuable asset to your husband.'

'Don't tease me, please.'

'I'm sorry if I offended you...but that's what most girls love to do, as soon as they get out of school.'

'May be. But I certainly am not one of them,' the girl said firmly. Then, with an abrupt change of mood, she smiled somewhat artificially. 'Okay, gentleman. I guess now you've the whole picture about me.'

'Not unless you tell me what made you run away from marriage.'

'So, you want to know all the whys and hows?'

'Just curious...'

The girl grimaced. Then, strolling down memory lane, she recalled, 'Well, I had just turned thirteen – a nervous teenager...' Stumbling over her words for a fraction of a second, she went on enchantedly, 'I was packed off to a boarding school in the States. There I lived and loved my six, eventful, teen years in hostels, except, of course, for short holiday breaks in India. I grew and matured with other girls of the same type and yet so different. Six years flashed past in one long band of happiness, joy, tears, sweat and fun.' Striving to make a favourable impression on me, she was speaking slowly, the words keeping pace with her memories. 'Back home after graduation, my suitcases were not even unpacked yet, when imagine, my parents received a proposal for my hand. How disrupting!'

'Why is that disrupting?'

'You see, I cannot allow myself to depart from my plans,' she spoke as if in self-defence.

'Of course not.'

My unthinking support made the America-returned girl, more glib.

'Parties and picnics, dramas and discos, singing and dancing, swimming and yatching, golfing and riding, trekking and skating...'

'Hold it! Hold it!' My mind was confused over her boasting. Her Yankee drawl, outlook and ways, her carefree conversation and varied interests, were pointing to one direction – an Indian turned American.

'You might say it is madness to have so many interests, but they're all equally important to me.'

'Say no more, I'm convinced.'

'Well, those were my plans before leaving the States. But no sooner had I set foot in Bombay, than, the shocking news came.'

'That's how life is. You plan something and someone else comes from behind, to upset it. It always happens.'

'But my parents were very happy about it.'

'Because all your plans were upset?'

'No, no. Not for that. Because the proposal was from a most eligible bachelor.'

'Good cometh out of the evil. The Bible may be old, but is a mine of gold.'

'Aren't you curious to know about him?'

'I guess I ought to be, but I'm not.'

Although mildly disappointed, she gave me a sweet smile.

'I thought you would ask the question that everybody asks.'

'I'm sorry,' I apologised with masked sarcasm. 'How thoughtless of me.' And then, relenting to her thinking and dramatising, in a honeyed voice I asked, 'Would you please tell me who's that eligible bachelor?'

Trying hard to sound factual, she replied, 'A young millionaire.'

'Wheeeeee! A young millionaire!'

'What is there to be so excited?'

'Lucky girl,' struggling to conceal my excitement, I said, 'only a young millionaire can provide more money than his wife can spend.'

She smiled faintly. 'It's natural for anyone to disbelieve. But then why should I waste your time talking about it.'

'No, please go on,' I said heartily. 'I'm all ears.'

For over a minute she looked thoughtful, then signed.

'All right, good man, if you insist.'

'Please start from the beginning.'

'Need I begin right from my birth?'

'I don't want you to be so elaborate.'

'Just how much?'

'As much as you think is necessary.'

'That's a little better.' Before starting, she cleared her throat. 'Well, listen, then...'

Half a minute elapsed but she couldn't get a single word out. Predictably, she was considering how much she would give out.

It was long overdue, when I broke in, just to feel her pulse.

'If it is something that you don't want to reveal, you don't have to.'

'Nothing like that, thank you. But I'd like to ask you something, if I may.'

'Please do.'

After some thought, she said, 'Can you stand the idea of being betrothed today and married off, tomorrow?'

'No. I cannot. That's a gross injustice,' I commiserated.

'So, when I learnt about that, at breakfast on a Sunday, in July last, I protested desperately...' her voice dropped an octave and lost volume.

She was silent for a minute, recollecting the particular incident of her life, that had happened some months ago.

Longing to listen to her story, I leaned back comfortably in my seat, while she flashbacked.

'Marriage? Oh no! In an era when many of my contemporaries are dreaming of flying in space, piloting jet fighters, becoming Supreme Court justices, network television anchors and big city police chief, etc., you expect me to get married! Oh Mamma, I'm only nineteen and that is no age for marriage.'

'Nineteen is no age for marriage!' echoed Mummy. 'Some still choose full-time motherhood and home making.'

'A bit surprised! All the more shocking that my mother, like most mothers, is also a staunch believer in the myth, that the only proper role for a daughter is to 'grow up' and become a 'full woman' by getting married, rearing children and serving her family. All other doors are closed. But the point is, being an educated girl from an urban, affluent family, am I not entitled to a choice?

'Be fair, Mom. For years I was in the States, mugging books and worrying about my results. I'm back home for a few days only and you're all set to get me married! Let me catch my breath. Give me time to get the feel of life in Bombay and then, I shall let you know if I'm ready for marriage.'

'Will the proposal wait for you till then?'

'Who cares! *Naa to naa sahi*!'

'And where will we find another boy like Ronen?'

'He needn't be another Ronen. And, to believe there's only one Ronen is fairytale stuff, Mom. Whatever happens, for another two years, I don't want to marry.'

'It's a painful decision.' Grandma's comment only encouraged Mummy, who hastened to complain.

'Ma, your loving pet is unmanageable. Is this what you desired in return for her expensive, American education?'

Grandma smiled: 'Why find fault with the American education? This is a phase every teenager goes through. You worry unnecessarily. Significantly, what both of you argued about, sounds right. But remember, just as a lime, when squeezed too hard and for too long, loses its lemony taste and turns bitter, likewise, if you pressurise someone to do something against their will, it would result in revolt. Especially in marriage, we've to renounce the use of force. For, a forced marriage does not last. Moreover, she is old enough to take her own decision. If you don't mind, please back off and leave my granddaughter alone. Don't make it further difficult for me, to lift the gloom that has settled over the mother-daughter relationship.' Grandma, always friendly and helpful, a source of encouragement and sympathy, soothed her daughter-in-law.

Mummy felt immensely relieved, knowing everything would be well taken care of, by grandma. Then, saying, 'as you wish', she rose to her feet and was gone, too quickly, but happy.

Now, alone with grandma, her eyes fixed steadily on me, I found it hard to continue the conversation. While she waited for a logical opening, I played with my cup and saucer.

However, before long, I found my voice.

'Grandma,' coming right to the point, I ventured, 'you shouldn't rush me into marriage just because I am past eighteen.'

'Can't help it. It's a must, for a girl of our family.'

I did not take grandma's reply seriously, so I joked, 'Gone are the days when women were considered suitable only for motherhood and homemaking. If only my grandmother could forget her outdated prejudices.'

'Even then, a girl or our family must be married while she is in her teens.'

'That's not fair.'

'No, probably not. Nor I am trying to be unfair. I am only trying to knock some good sense into your immature head.'

Stunned, I gave her a dumb, disbelieving stare. Grandma had closed her eyes, as though there was nothing more to be said, on the subject.

Several silent moments later, I heard myself saying, 'That's the penalty for my being a girl, I suppose?'

Grandma opened her grey eyes and watching me closely for a longer moment said, 'Don't say penalty. That's for keeping up the family tradition.'

'To be married in one's teens? If you were all that keen on having me married in my teens, then why was I sent to study abroad? You should have tied my hands and feet together and thrown me into the Arabian Sea.'

'No matter how far you've distanced yourself from the family, it is a misfortune to inherit no traditions. The most graceful people in the world are following long practised traditions they have inherited and grown used to.'

'The traditions have had their time, grandma. The new generation gives no importance to hoary traditions. Today, they're being broken even in remote villages. The past must give way to the present.'

'Like most teenagers, you're arguing to assert you independence.'

'Being a Harvard graduate, I hate to be categorised into the set of "most teenagers". I'm a young adult, able to take care of myself and I want to know about myself. Tell me, grandma, how can I make you understand that I'm not interested in marriage now?'

'The most frightening aspect of growing up, is self-exploration. It's terrifying, but it teaches you about yourself. I'm afraid you may do something foolish – short of running away from home. So, think it over once again and you may find a reason to change your mind. All I'm saying is, give it a try, for no one's sake but your own.'

The argument wheeled back to where it had started, leaving me with no choice but to bluff.

And I did.

'Grandma, yesterday I came across a news item that our Parliament is soon going to pass an Act fixing twenty-one years as the minimum marriage age for girls, to check population growth.'

'I do not read all the gossip in the newspapers,' Grandma said. 'Nor do I believe in such Acts. I think it is impractical. Just by raising the legal age to twenty-one, there is no guarantee that the family will have fewer children.'

'Grandma, suppose – just suppose – the Act is passed; what would you do then? Postpone marriage?'

'No', was grandma's chilling reply.

'Tell me honestly, grandma, what do you have against me?'

Grandma was silent for a moment.

'Nothing. I've nothing against you, child. I simply want you to understand me and what I think about our family traditions.'

'Tradition, tradition, tradition. You're overflowing with inherited traditions. Please grandma, stop saying that again and again. A decade ago, the decision not to tie the knot was a difficult one for women, but today, it's a matter of will.'

'This isn't as crazy as it seems. The male has less to lose than the female, who tends to be left with the job of bearing and rearing the children, which should make women instinctively more discerning. Now that we are in a position to make our own decisions, we should put pressure on making it happen.'

The explosion I had expected, did not come. Although grandma was hurt, she spoke in an easy, conversational tone.

'Culture and custom are interrelated. When these two are in alignment inside the hearts and minds of people of the land, tradition takes root, spreading all over. It develops into a permanent system.

'To bring about a change in deep-rooted tradition, is a Herculean task. You just cannot abolish a system or legislate a change in culture. A lot of people, over time, have become dependent on old cultures and systems and it takes a lot of courage to change the structures and systems. And, yes, each generation does have the right to demand some changes.' Coming forward, grandma suddenly took me into her arms and planted a kiss on my forehead. 'You're an intelligent young woman and a lot of your objections to teen marriage make sense. Anyway, I'm not going to advise you, or spoil your day, by debating whether tradition is outdated or not. Enough arguments can still be made, against or for it. If you like, we shall talk more about it, tonight.'

'Thank you, grandma, for your willingness to discuss the old wrongs and ultimately eliminate them, where necessary.'

'That night, after dinner, we resumed to settle the long-debated subject. My grandma, an attractive mix of tradition and modernity, kept trying to reason with me but I stood my ground.' She concluded.

'But where did the battle of tradition versus modernism end?' I asked her, with some trepidation.

'Well, good man, I requested grandma to give me some time to learn a few things about life.'

'Time given?'

'One year. On condition that I remained engaged to him,' she said, with an answering smile.

With a newfound feeling of independence, the poor, little, rich girl, felt she was getting along quite well in her rebellion.

'I assume, then, Miss Independent, you're in your own world of true freedom.'

'Yeah, as free as a bird in a tree.'

'No boundaries?'

'Of course, there are. Even freedom has to have some boundaries. Freedom does not mean doing everything we want.'

'Could you elaborate on this?'

'Well, we all know freedom is an essential part of human life. It's a necessity. We also know, freedom without any restriction, can be misused. Of all living creatures, only birds and animals enjoy unlimited freedom. But we are not birds and animals we're human beings. For generations we're known by family names and each individual member is answerable for the whole family. Freedom, therefore, is limited by sensible restrictions. Get what I mean?'

'Yes, I get you. But being away from home, who is there now to check you?'

'Why, myself. After all, I share the fair name of our family, don't I?'

'That's true. Freedom is fine as long as you don't abuse it.'

'It's also true that all grown-up boys and girls should be free to make their own decisions and even to commit their own mistakes.'

Then what are parents for? Don't parents have any responsibility for the grown-ups?'

'Well, parents cannot be with them everywhere, throughout twenty-four hours of the day.'

'Possibly impossible.'

'I'm glad,' repressing a sly smile, she said, 'you're beginning to understand the modern family technology.'

Seizing her own sarcasm to use against her, I replied, 'The credit goes to the teacher.'

Outplayed, she blinked at me for a long moment, as if she had only just seen me. But from the innocent expression of a small boy on my face, she knew at once what role the situation demanded of her and, eventually she snapped, at me, in a sharp, tutorial voice:

'Have you done homework?'

'No, teacher,' I replied sheepishly in a little boy voice.

'Why? Why is it not done?'

Inaudibly muttering, 'Sorry, teacher,' I broke into tears, the way a seven-year-old schoolboy, would.

My pretence fittingly matched hers. She spurted with musical laughter.

'Am I forgiven, teacher?' With pleading eyes, I looked up at her earnestly.

'Yes,' she said with an air of boundless generosity, 'you're forgiven.'

'Thank you, teacher.'

Both of us drained of pretences, were now fighting very hard not to laugh, and then, to our own surprise, we collapsed into each other's arms, laughing hysterically.

Into this joyous moment, a deep voice intruded:

'Ticket please.'

Didn't hope that the privacy of a coupe would be invaded by a TTE (Travelling Ticket Examiner) and the fun would be so short-lived. However, standing awkwardly apart, I produced the tickets for his perusal.

My companion sat huddled in the corner, as far as the seat permitted, but the wish at the back of her mind just then was, to wring the intruder's neck.

'I apologise for intruding.' The TTE handed the tickets back to me and turned to the door.

'Next time don't walk in, without knocking on the door.' That was a soft warning from my travelling companion.

The TTE turned back. 'There won't be a next time, Madame. Honeymooners are exempted from such disturbances.' Courteously raising his cap, he slipped away.

The word 'honeymooners' irritated her. 'What nonsense!' She hissed, darting an angry look at the closing door.

The way we two, so young, were laughing in each other's arms, it was logical to take us for honeymooners. I, a misfit in this role, couldn't help but laugh at my companion's unfounded anger.

That annoyed her. 'I could understand it if you had told the TTE about our relationship, instead of laughing like a fool.'

'Then he would have got us into serious trouble.'

'How?'

'By informing the police.'

'Don't try to scare me, it won't work.'

'You're forgetting one thing, Madam. This is not America. This is India.'

The tongue-lasher made a face and turned her back – a sign that told me, to stop.

Four

So I stopped

Thereafter, a good many minutes passed without any conversation.

In this period of transition, to keep my mind occupied, I unfolded the morning newspaper and made well-intentioned attempts to read the lighter sections. But the letters seemed to dance in rhythm with the clanging of the train.

My charming companion, unpredictable and full of surprises, had lapsed into silence. Silence being the solution to everything, probably, she had found peace in it. And in her abstracted state, she made herself at home, by crossing one smooth leg over the other, cocking her head to one side, shutting her eyes and pretending to be oblivious to the chugging of the train, as if in meditation.

For hours now, we were travelling together, but did not know each other's name. This was in my mind like itches, that needed to be scratched.

After a minute's hesitation, with a soft touch on her arm, I whispered: 'Eh-eh-eh...Will you ever tell me your name?'

My intrusion into her meditation only filled her with disgust.

As I braced myself for the inevitable barrage of bitter words, her eyes flashing annoyance, seemed to warn me: *stop that eh, eh, will you?*

Mumbling nervously, 'Until now, I don't know your name...' I risked a glance at those critical eyes, staring at me in the face.

The delicate moment was getting worse by the second when, unwillingly, she gave her name in a half-whisper, 'Dolly' and slipped back to her previous, meditating state.

Till yesterday, she had taught in a girls' school and had lived in the hostel. But now she was in a train, far from the hostel. For a moment, just for a moment, she wanted to be there....

Gradually, the long hours that separated her from the students began disappearing and memories, sweet and sour, began to replay through her mind, in slow motion, giving her a chance to observe each detail as if she were a spectator watching herself.

It was a Monday morning, two months after her joining the school as a primary level teacher. As Dolly entered the classroom, the monitor greeted her with a rose bouquet:

'Happy Birthday to you!'

'Oh, thank you sweethearts.' It was the instant reaction of Dolly, who was deeply moved by the pleasant surprise. Then there was a scramble to offer the red roses to their loving teacher. It was a never-seen-before 'Happy Birthday', of any teacher.

When the students were back at their places, Dolly expressed her deep gratitude and regret:

'I had totally forgotten about it. Thank you very much for remembering your teacher's birthday. But I haven" got any sweets to give you.'

'Don't you worry, Miss. I got it for you.' The monitor, who was the teacher's pet, brought out a carton of milk chocolates. Giving one to her teacher, she placed the carton on the table and imperiously directed the class to pick up – one each.

In a matter of minutes, the carton was empty.

Now, chocolate bar in hand, the whole class stood up, waiting in silence.

As Dolly bit her chocolate bar, all the students bit theirs. Then the fun started.

'It's bitter!' the monitor said loudly.

'Make it sweet!' the whole class demanded unanimously.

Guided by an unknown instinct, Dolly kissed the monitor who was standing by her side.

'That's for the monitor. How about us?' The girls appealed.

A hunger for their teacher's birthday kiss was glinting in their eyes, and that propelled Dolly to go round, kissing chubby cheeks, one by one.

The Principal, a Parsi lady, who was a savage disciplinarian, was in her early fifties. She was on her first round of the day. The clip-clop, clip-clop of her high-heeled shoes, stopped at the corridor. Standing by the window she saw what was going on in the class. Returning to her office she demanded Dolly's immediate presence, through the intercom.

The moment Dolly stepped into the office, the Principal's grave voice boomed: 'Do you know why I have called you?'

Speechless, she stared at her.

'Any lesson imparted during the past half-hour since school started?' The Principal wanted to know.

Dolly said nothing.

'You are a teacher, come here to teach, not to play. Don't let me remind you this simple thing again.'

'Sorry, Madam.'

'No apology needed. You can go now.'

Ten days later, Dolly had her second warning, a severe one.

The Principal was busy talking to a visitor in her office. Through the open windows came floating peals of silvery laughter. She was interrupted by another laughing fit, a much longer one than the last. It went on and on. It seemed there would be no end to it.

'Excuse me,' she said to the visitor and dashed for the classroom, from where the shrieks and laughs of children were emanating. At the door, flabbergasted, she stopped, finding the class teacher also spluttering, in fits of laughter.

'Ooops! A nervous whisper from the backbencher, whom nobody heard. Her furtive entry however, was picked up by the sensitive eardrum of the monitor, who, in turn, alerted the class, losing no time.

'The Principal!'

A shocked silence fell.

Students hold their breath… their heads sharply turned to the door, where the Principal stood, with her eyes fixed severely on their teacher.

'I have told you already, Miss Dolly, not to indulge children so much; but you don't care.'

A deep sense of humiliation had turned Dolly wooden. When she was able to speak, she said, 'I'm sorry, Madam.'

'You ought to be ashamed of yourself. And you call yourself a teacher, Miss Dolly!'

Clip-clop, clip-clop, the Principal went away. Every clip-clop of her high-heeled shoes intensified her anger.

This can't go on, Dolly thought. Sooner or later, I'll have to leave and it might as well be now...

On the spur of the moment, she wrote out the resignation letter. But a prudent insight into the momentous decision changed her mind. Yet, it was quite some time before she could continue with the class again.

As was bound to happen sooner or later, Dolly's teaching career came to an end, after twenty days.

A pin-drop silence pervaded the examination hall. It was the last day of the first term. Supervisors had positioned themselves. One of them was Dolly.

No indiscipline was in sight. Every pen was busy writing.

'Either the papers are very easy or the children are exceptionally bright,' Dolly mused. But, towards the end of the day, she spotted something abnormal, when the other supervisor settled down for a quiet doze.

Taking advantage of the relaxed vigilance, a ninth standard girl was inching the book closer to her, from under the desk. Looking around cautiously, she started copying. Not walking straight to her, Dolly went round and stood behind the girl, noiselessly. Giving her sufficient time to copy, she placed a hand gently on her shoulder. Panic gripped the girl. She half-turned, supporting her elbows on the desk.

'After the examination see me in the staff room, without fail.' Not harsh, or rude, or severe, but a mild order that must be obeyed. She then walked away with the book.

In the staff room, Dolly was waiting for the girl. Half a dozen teachers were busy gossiping.

When the bell rang to mark the end of the examination, everyone sighed, amid happy smiles, except the girl who was caught copying, red-handed. A while later, eyes downcast with shame, she stood before Dolly, while others stared at her curiously. Unmindful of their presence, Dolly looked her up and down.

Fearing the worst, the girl trembled. But Dolly had no intention of exposing her. Without referring to the incident, she handed back the book saying, 'Fool! I thought how could you have forgotten this?'

The well-meant words had a double meaning, which the girl understood. 'It won't happen again,' she wanted to say. But Dolly's calmness and few words had rendered her speechless.

These days' *chamchas* are everywhere. Even in the teacher's group there was one, who at once reported the incident to the Principal.

In the Principal's office, Dolly was summoned to explain under what authority she had let the cheat go, unpunished.

'A long brutal lecture or even worse, threats of debarring her from examinations wouldn't help change her mind.'

'You should have reported to me first, instead of deciding yourself.'

'I thought it better that way.'

'You thought it better. Your way was ignoring the Principal! Such behaviour does not befit you.'

'In other words, whatever I do, is wrong.'

'Don't take the liberty of taking decisions. Such trespassing I don't appreciate.'

'Where I don't have independent thinking, freedom to do the right things, there I don't see my future.'

'So?'

Dolly, welcoming the opportunity, quickly produced an envelope from her handbag. 'Madam will surely find it worth appreciating.'

'What's this?'

'My resignation.'

At first, the Principal was somewhat astounded by her pomposity. Then murmuring 'It's madness,' she began to open the envelope.

Sad incidents inscribed on her soul, Dolly was lying in her berth, curled up like a cat, when she drifted off, into an uneasy sleep.

Five

Suddenly, I found myself isolated.

To help pass the time, I attempted first to doze, then reached for a book. It wasn't just any book. It was a jet-paced, political thriller, and the more I read, the more interesting I found it.

When Dolly awoke from her trance, I had already read a good many pages and had become utterly absorbed.

Now sitting bolt upright, first she stretched, did a few arm bends, then shook her head most vigorously, to banish the bitter-sweet memories of her short, teaching days. Finally, in an attempt to draw my attention, she lightly tapped my arm.

Distracted, I slammed the book shut and looked up.

'Good man, mind telling me where we're going?' Seeing the frown on my face intensifying, she added thickly, 'I've a right to know.'

'Do you?'

'Shouldn't I know where you're taking me?'

Detecting a smirk on her face, I countered, 'What do you mean, *taking* you? You make it sound like a kidnapping.'

'Only this time,' she interrupted, laughing, 'the captor paid the victim the ransom.'

'When the victim is a good conversationalist, the captor is helpless.'

'Stop that crap and tell me, where are we going?' Suddenly, she switched back to where it had all started.

'Mandu.'

'What remains there, now?'

'Plenty.'

'Huh, those romantic monuments?'

'Besides monuments, there are forts, palaces, havelis, tombs... in fact, history awaits you at every turn. The great Shah Jahan was inspired enough, to send his chief architect to Mandu, to see Hosang Shah's tomb, before designing the Taj Mahal.'

'That's history!'

'To neglect history is not prudent.'

'Hey,' she made a sudden somersault, 'you're an architect, aren't you?'

For a while I wondered what she could have seen of an architect in me.

'Aren't you?' Once more, she asked, brimming with confidence.

The stupid question disgusted me and I looked away.

'I cannot be wrong... I cannot be wrong,' she boasted. Then, in support of her claim, she added, 'Mathematician, poet, philosopher, scientist, playwright, teacher, painter, writer, singer... I can identify them, just like that.'

The way she said this, by snapping her fingers, made me want to slap her, but I resisted the urge, because that would be too harsh. Only later did I discover that I was still boiling inside and trying not to show it. I said, with controlled mildness, 'But it is not all that easy to identify a classical idiot.'

'Why do you denigrate yourself? You are good looking enough, to be an architect.'

'So?'

'So you have more of a right to be one, than anybody else.'

'Do I really look that good?'

'You sure do.'

'I'm gratified, Miss America, for passing my looks for an architect.'

Wasting the looks-bait she had thrown at me, she now came up, with a face-saving lie. 'Honestly, I wasn't criticising.'

My resentful voice blew the lid off her sense mechanism. With all circuits snapping to life, she hastened to give the tension a soothing wipe.

'Just as the shortest distance between two points is a straight line, the quickest route to friendship, between two persons, is admiration.'

Pretending to be highly impressed by the geometrical simile, I said, 'A teacher is always right.'

Understandably, my friendship was as necessary for her, as safety. But, for moulding companionship into friendship, it takes time. Finding success there, Dolly shrank into herself, contemplating her next move. I returned to the book, lighting a cigarette.

The train was now passing through an attractive, scenic route. I turned a page, flicking ash off my cigarette. Absorbed in reading I became oblivious to everything else.

Time dragged on.

As the iron horse leapt past a station, a chord of rejection twinged in, catapulting her into mischief. She gave my thigh a stinging squeeze, for attention. Her idiocy cut no ice with me and it made her desperate. Flouting all norms, she snatched the book from my hand.

Unable to bear this errant nonsense, I looked sternly at her face. At once she dropped the book, which missing my lap, fell onto my knee and slid down the leg, to the floor.

My hand reached down, trembling with anger. While inching closer to the book, she lurched forward and fell over me. Our heads bumped and an invisible charge, passed between us.

Dolly, tense and uncomfortable, I, shocked and confused, looked at each other for a split second. And then, started laughing.

Laugh. Laugh. Laugh. Laugh.

When the laugh had quietened itself, almost immediately, the teenage chatterbox tried to draw me into a conversation.

'Excuse my asking, good man.'

'I object to being called good man!'

'What shall I call you then?'

'Sanchu.'

'Sanchu,' she mouthed my name softly, as though it were honey-sweet, to utter.

'And one more thing, stop asking questions.'

'Mister Sanchu, remember your word.' She repeated what I had said to her, a little while ago. 'As companions, we must know each other a little more than strangers.'

'Yes, I did say that.'

'Then how can you prevent me from asking questions?'

A face so naturally beautiful. Then, as if not believing, I found a startling contrast in that perfect face. Beneath her artless, childlike simplicity and her matchless beauty, she was shrewd, quick-tempered, sharp-tongued and, in her own way, bold.

'All right, Miss, ask anything.'

'Anything I like?'

'Anything you like.'

Her dark, deep eyes, regarded me with suspicion for a few moments. Then she smiled sweetly. 'I've told everything you wanted to know about me. Now tell me about yourself; your background, your ambition, you struggle...'

'It can shock or irritate you,' I warned her.

'I don't care. Shoot. I'm shockproof.'

'Well...'

'If you feel ashamed to tell, then you don't have to.'

'No, I don't even feel ashamed to admit that I'm not a Harvard graduate. I can't sing and I can't dance. I don't have time for dramas and discos, movies and concerts. And about riding-motoring-hiking-golfing-rowing-shooting, those extreme luxuries, I can't even dream of. My life is not as glamorous as yours.'

Oh oh, don't tell me about your don'ts. Tell me, what do you do, other than visiting historical places?'

'I write.'

My reply, without any emphatic brevity, sounded so insane that her gradually penetrating eyes, seemed to examine every pore in my face.

'I write, means not just write; I am a writer.'

'Oh,' she flashed a smile. 'Everybody thinks he or she can be a writer.'

'Go ahead, say it,' I teased her, 'Say that you've always wanted to be a writer.'

'Don't tell me it's a crime to try.'

'It's a crime to think it's easy.'

'Any fool knows that.'

'If you didn't have such a beautiful face,' patting her on the cheek I said, 'I'd suspect you of making fun of me.'

'When a writer cannot desist himself from granting undue concession to a beautiful face, he's done for.'

It was the last thing I expected to hear and it made me explode into real laughter.

'Stop laughing. It's as pointless as it is distasteful.'

When I was still laughing, she was sharpening her tongue for a deadly attack and eventually she did. 'It's a pleasure to talk to a writer,' she mocked gently. 'Are you really a good writer, or is the big ego a big bluff?'

'No bluff. I do write.'

'Okay, fine. You write. But what do you write? Children's textbooks, sports, travel, art, history, law, technology, polities, economics?' She reeled off randomly, names of various subjects, and I parried each one with negative headshakes.

'Then what?'

'Guess if you can,' I told her, letting the climax build up.

'It must be Cookery or Beauty care.'

'Those are the areas out of bounds for men.'

'Nonsense. Gender has nothing to do with subject matter.'

'If what you say is right, then I must be wrong,' I compromised, managing my best smile.

'Okay, okay. Now tell me, what have you written?'

'Three novels.'

'You're a novelist!' Surprised, she asked herself, *'Why hadn't I thought of it?'* Then, fixing me with a benevolent look, she asked, 'Are you twenty-five yet?'

'I'll be twenty-four, in twenty days' time.'

Evidently, it amazed her that one as young as myself had written three novels. Soon, however, amazement dissolved and praise oozed out, from every pore of the beautiful face. 'God, you must be a genius.'

'Not at all,' I said. But I liked the praise. It warmed me inside.

'Of course you are. Who can deny you that credit? After all, you have a learned opus to write.'

'It'll make you laugh; so far, not even one has been published.'

'Not even one?'

'Not even one,' I echoed shyly.

'And you claim you're a writer?'

'I do not claim anything. I only stated a fact.'

'What's the matter?' She asked suddenly serious. 'Did you ever try with any publisher?'

'Many. But its my luck that the frustration and pressure come in form of rejection slips: We cannot use it but we loved reading it. try us again sometime.'

'Luck is no reason.'

'What I mean is, they just don't care for a struggling aspirant.'

'No. It must be something else.'

'Or may be because I don't write commercial tripe.'

'There you are. Can't you write commercial tripe?'

'Anybody can, but I don't want to.'

'And why not?'

'Because I cannot mix business with my writing.'

'Suppose you could bend your principle a little...?'

'Impossible.'

'I admire a man of principles but for attracting readers, it's time you learnt a few useful tips on novel writing.' For far too long, Dolly's piercing eyes studied me, with icy calm. But when she found expression, it was simply a friendly advice. 'Money and crime make an explosive mixture, Mr Sanchu. Mix them with sex and you get a big bonfire. Those kinds of novels are much in demand these days. Try your hand today and you will be a rich man tomorrow.'

'Thanks a lot for those hot tips but I'll never use them. I'm sorry, Dolly. I'm just not cut out, to be a fast buck writer.'

My lively companion, corrupted by American notions, shrank like a pricked balloon. 'As a writer, I should give the readers what is good for them, not what they want.'

'Writers are paranoids,' she said sadly. 'God knows when they will learn to be practical, by which I mean money-wise.'

'You're breaking your head for nothing. I'm not hankering after riches.'

'Be realistic, man!' Dolly urged. 'For all good writing there must be peace. And peace can be had through financial independence only.'

'In a sense, yes.'

'This means, a lot depends on the sale of the book.'

'To some extent, yes.'

'Well, then, Mr Writer, you should look into the interest and tastes of the buying public.'

'Compromise on my principles? Never!'

'Toss your ego in the wastebasket or else you'll never write a best-selling novel. A heavy, literary book is boring and elitist and does not sell. I am not advocating a reduction in quality, but just stressing on what the public wish to read.'

'Thank you very much for this piece of advice. But I don't like people telling me what to write and how to go about it.'

'Those are tall talks. Meaningless. Useless. Nonsensical.' She hit me with barbed words. 'You must accept the fact that when a customer spends money on a book, the writer makes a contract to entertain him, failing which, he ends up a scribbler.'

'Very well, madam, I am not a writer. I am a scribbler.'

Not content, the cynic sneered. 'And what do you think a publishing house is, a charitable organisation?'

There was a pause and she saw that she had gone too far. She breathed deeply and fell silent.

The silence lasted for some more time.

'What's a writer, by the way?' I smiled at her, with the pride of a creative writer.

'There're innumerable writers from various fields. It is not easy to standardise one from the other. Could you be specific?'

'One who writes novels, I mean, a creative writer.'

'To describe a creative writer off hand, is exceedingly difficult.' She laughed with girlish embarrassment and added quickly, 'I cannot find the right words, but in precise form...in my own words if I may...'

'Yes, yes. Say it in your own words,' I goaded her.

'Well...' Dipping into her storehouse of literal wisdom, she said, 'All writers are jugglers. They juggle with words.'

The condensed interpretation, flavoured with humour, made me laugh.

'What could that laugh mean but a mockery of me?'

'No-no. Nothing of the sort. On the contrary, you're partly right. I award you pass marks.'

'Oh! That's more than enough.' Her eyes danced with enthusiasm. 'Believe me, throughout my student career, I fared no better. I passed all the exams on the borderline, only. Just one or two marks, here or there, would have been enough to tip the balance the other way.'

'By heaven, how dangerous were those years!'

'Good man, I love danger.'

'No doubt, you do.' A thinly disguised sarcasm in my voice went unnoticed.

'You know,' she then opted to explain, 'there is no advantage in being a borderline student. Nobody dares to overtake you.'

'May be, I don't know.'

'But you know a lot about the mode of writing, don't you?'

The tongue twister challenged me, tight-lipped and angry.

'Well...'

My hesitation delighted her. Her beautiful eyes puckered up for some mischief, as I met them.

'Don't think I'm trying to evaluate you, Sanchu.'

'I'm not worth trying, madam. But, I've a feeling that you can explain it better.'

'Well,' pondering for a long moment, she hit on an answer. 'I think a novel should be about life, or a segment of it and its main function is communication.'

'But if it communicates nothing, or different things to different people, what is its worth?'

'The answer in one word is: S-C-R-A-P.'

'For which a writer, a man of words, has only to aim at excellence. Unlike painting, dance or music, the written word has no direct appeal to our senses. Therefore, to add spice to his prose, a writer often chooses words that are a little out of the ordinary. It is the purest, intellectual exercise, in artistic creativity.'

My reply quietened her for some time. Slowly, she returned to the topic, with a different verve.

'I know, now I know.'

'What?'

'That some day, you're going to be a great novelist.'

The Adam-teaser gave me the pinprick, yet my mind refused to repay her.

'I appreciate the compliment, but I'm afraid you're overstating it a little.'

'Being polite doesn't mean you aren't great.'

'Don't flatter me. You know, great writers are rarely born. Then, if they are born, they become known late.'

'An honest writer wouldn't praise himself.' She flashed a dazzling smile.

While she waited, watching my reaction, silence stood guard between us.

Yet it was Dolly, who, changing her track, made a sudden switch to history, from literature.

'We've wasted too much time evaluating a creative writer and his writings. For a change, let's talk about Mandu, the historical place where we're going.'

It was her pattern of quarrel and compromise, repulse and surrender, argument and agreement, praise and censure. Also, this was her pattern of making a spontaneous choice of another subject of any kind, and it mattered very little with her. In the same vein she could debate geography or philosophy, chemistry or poultry, culture or vulture, dog or cat, God or demon, literature or furniture, from A to Z. Rather, she was a skilful debater, with a gift of the gab.

Caught up in her complex web of outstanding qualities while I was suffocating, she herself bailed me out.

'Now, you don't need to be a historian to enlighten me about Mandu.'

'Frankly speaking, since you brought up this topic, you should start.'

'Oh, come on. Be a sport.'

Determined not to concede, I snubbed her with a cold 'Sorry'. But she was impervious to snubs.

'Believe me, Sanchu, if it weren't for you, I wouldn't have come.'

'It's no use jacking me up. You should bear in mind that you came on your own. Not even once did I ask you to come.'

She was smiling, though her eyes mirrored my annoyance.

'Let's get one thing straight, Miss Dolly,' I reiterated. 'No taboo. Nobody is taking anybody. We're just two tourists. There's no attachment. Right?'

'Oh Sanchu, my poor Sanchu!' Dolly's voice tinkled with laughter. 'What you must understand is, that we're discussing Mandu, not about ourselves.'

'Thanks for reminding me.'

'For some, it's necessary.'

'Oh, I see.'

'No, you don't see. If you did, you wouldn't take a trifle, so seriously.'

Sensing and relishing, my discomfort, Dolly chose not to delve on the subject further. 'Gentleman, if I now come back to the point and offer my honest and frank opinion about the historic place.'

'Depends on how much you know about the place.'

'Well...' her mouth curved into a sardonic smile. 'The limited knowledge that I recently acquired, studying Indian history in my free periods, during the short teaching days, is of no match for you.'

'Where on earth did you get the idea that one's knowledge has to match that of the other? As long as you don't exaggerate on purpose, it doesn't matter much, even if it is wide off the mark.'

'That's very kind of you.' There was a sparkle of wicked laughter in her eyes before she donated her scant knowledge. 'Mandu, once the citadel of joy, is a city of ruins today. Those ruins are now the abode of hundreds of tiny, screeching bats, frequently haunted by serpents and beasts. A deserted city, silent and weeping.'

'No,' I contradicted stoutly. 'Those ruins are the beauty of Mandu and constitute living pages of history, from the tenth to the eighteenth centuries. A city whose massive, beautiful architecture stands lost in time. Popular belief holds, that the melody of Rupmati, a common shepherd girl, who became a Queen, still echoes there, at times.'

'All rubbish! Nonsensical! The ruins do echo at night, but to the angry roar of tigers and panthers and the eerie call of the jackals. And, in a very childish way, she mimicked the angry roar of a tiger and a panther and the howl of a jackal. But her childishness had no effect on me.

'Before reaching Mandu, your ears have already started rumbling with the angry growls of animals. I wonder how you'd assess Rupmati's melody, when we actually reach there.'

'Oh, don't pose to be so damned superior,' she said snootily. 'As a female, I can assess the graveness of Rupmati's melodies much more than you imagine. Besides, there is no difference between Rupmati and me.'

'No difference?'

'A little.'

'Exactly how little is little?'

She caught the instant interest in my voice.

'Well, the little difference between the two is,' she heaved a deep sigh, 'Rupmati is the forgotten past and Dolly is the living present.'

This parable, so solemnly said, saddened me.

'I'm so sorry. Never knew you had reached the end so early.'

'You needn't be sorry, Sanchu,' she said with a grave little smile on her face. After a slight pause, she resumed pensively, 'Love and marriage rarely go together. It's rare rarity.' She drew a long breath, like a sigh and turned her eyes to the receding wheat fields outside.

My most amusing companion was soon lost in a world of her own. At nineteen, she was already wise and well versed with life. She wasn't quick to give her identity, or her heart.

Six

While we were trying to know each other, we were still talking non-stop, ricocheting from one subject to another, the Express made an unscheduled halt at a small station.

Instantly, the quiet platform hummed with activity. Vendors, outshouting one another, screamed in their raucous voice.

I leaned out of the window and bought a packet of salted cashewnuts. As I popped some into my mouth, I heard my name being called. Who could it be, in a place so alien? I pricked up my ears to hear it for a second time.

Before I could hear it again, my wandering eyes spotted a man in the distance, whose face couldn't be seen clearly. He was rushing towards me. Then, one close look at him and I knew him to be Inder, the bearded artist, as shabby, long haired and grubby, as ever. He came to me straight, held my face with both hands and gave me a smacking kiss. It was an act that suggested that he had found his long-lost little brother.

Dolly, sitting as still as a mouse, watched the crazy proceedings in amusement.

'How the devil did you land here?'

'Why, didn't the imp remember me?' Countered Inder and we rumbled with laughter.

No laugh. Not even a bit of a smile did my friend get, from my companion, who made a wry face instead. That was Dolly.

'Jokes aside, where are you off to?' I asked Inder.

'Where do you think I may be going?'

'No idea.'

'There's nothing to hide from you, *yaar*,' said Inder with a touch of sadness. 'My ailing mother is undergoing treatment in the district hospital, seven miles away from here. Her condition is very serious. Anything can happen to her, any moment.' His voice quavered, with his eyes beginning to get tearful.

'Don't talk like that. There's always hope. You should think about good things. What is she suffering from?'

'She is sick as hell. Her heart is very weak, chest pains and shortness of breath.'

'I'm sorry to hear that, Inder.'

Wiping a tear from his eye, he said, 'I'm afraid this could well be our last meeting.'

'Don't worry. She is still alive and life means hope.'

Even while sympathising, I was studying Inder's face and found him transparently honest. In the past, on one or two occasions, he did play tricks, to swindle money. But no, not this time.

'How much money do you have, in your pocket now?' I asked bluntly.

His fingers curled uncertainly around a few coins in his pocket before taking his first glance at Dolly. 'Your girlfriend, eh?'

'Don't bother, *yaar*,' looking obliquely at my companion, I replied. 'She's just a fellow passenger.'

Dolly heard me and rolled her eyeballs heavenwards, seeking truth in my pronouncement.

'Why don't you come down, *yaar*. After all, this is going to be a private talk between two pals.'

'Sure.'

Going over to the platform, as I stood lighting a cigarette, my friend put his arm around my shoulder and spoke in whispers, 'I've only two rupees in my pocket.' He attempted a smile, but it was bleak.

'I guessed as much.'

'What do I care now that I've met you?'

'You don't have to butter me. Tell me how much you want.'

'How much can you spare?'

'Much depends on what you ask and what I have.'

For a second he rubbed his chin thoughtfully, 'Two hundred bucks will do.'

'Here's three hundred.' Thrusting three crisp hundred-rupee notes in his palm, I said, 'On reaching home, be sure to write about her health. Just in case you need more money, don't forget to add a line. By the end of this week, I'll be back in Delhi.'

First, he gave a grateful smile, then, pocketing the money, he hugged me. 'You're really a godsend friend.'

When the money was changing hands, Dolly's face showed a look of disgust, visibly unhappy with my friendly act.

Now, with the whistle of the train, we knew that time had run out and the meeting was over. But Inder still kept holding my hand and would not allow me to go. He was weeping.

As the train gradually accelerated, Dolly called out,

'Sanchu, if you don't come in at once, I'll pull the chain.'

Inder dropped my hand like a hot potato. Once freed, I jumped onto the footboard and waved him goodbye. But he kept waving to me, with tears in his eyes, until I lost sight of him. Then a dismal thought, that I was backing out, just when he needed me most, crept over me. Wishing we hadn't met, I cherished the thought within and returned to my berth.

'Was he also a writer?' asked Dolly, looking at my worried face.

'No. Painter.'

'I should have known it from his seedy appearance.'

'No comment, please. He is my friend and will always remain one.'

'In helping a friend, you are incredibly generous. Generosity is a fine thing. That doesn't mean you must part with so much money when we're out touring. Wouldn't we need more money than anybody else?' She scolded me with a patronising intimacy, that had no basis in our relationship.

Waving a hand in airy dismissal, I dragged on my cigarette.

She shrugged philosophically. 'Putting me off like that won't make the money grow in the purse. Well, they say,' she added with a chuckle, 'that a free spender grows poor by looking rich. Wise up, Sanchu, while there's still time, or you will be on the street, one day.'

'Mind your own business.'

'I can't unless you tell me what you do, for a living.'

'Do I have to?'

'Everyone does.'

'Miss, don't level me with everyone.'

'Sorry, tomorrow's great novelist cannot be everyone, but some special one.' Her eyes twinkled with sarcastic humour. 'So I suppose, a lot of your showing off was in conformation to your being Someone Special!'

'You're damn right! That's the sort of person I am.'

'Fine. Now I know why you spend money with childlike abandon. But where do you get it from?'

'I've a money plant.'

'Oon hoon!' She shook her head disapprovingly. Then, giving herself two or three seconds to think, she declared, 'Looks like you've tapped some hidden treasure.'

'You seem to be eaten up with curiosity; if only your words were true.'

The undisguised taunt dimmed her spirit. But her guess instinct still remained. While groping for another guess, suddenly her eyes sparkled. An instant later, she was clapping like a nine-year-old, bursting with pride and excitement.

'Whew! I got it!'

'Have you, really?' I was rather sceptical.

Nodding very slowly, she was about to come out with the fresh guess when a vexing thought furrowed her brows. For the first time she was showing a beginning to the end of her guess bid. But when she spoke, her voice was calm and certain.

'A generous document made you rich, overnight.'

'Yes, yes,' I egged her on. 'Keep guessing.'

This deflated the inexhaustible speculator, for a moment.

'Why? Didn't your heirless affluent distant relative provide for you a tidy sum in his will?'

'Pull the other one,' I told her jokingly.

'Jackpot?' As I nodded in negation, she said, 'Then it must be lottery.'

'No. I wouldn't accept it, even if you buy me the prize-winning ticket.'

'Sour grapes.'

'Money is sweet I know, but it's not important to me.'

'Admirable.' Even though she was thoroughly beaten, there was a hint of mockery in the voice.

'I think your guess basket is empty now.'

'Okay, Sanchu, I'm not going to bother you with guesses anymore. But what's your source of income?'

Trying to seem matter of fact, I said, 'I write speeches for politicians, irrespective of their party affiliations.'

'And what can it earn? Pats? Laurels? Thanks?' She needled, but that went into me like a dagger.

I respectably took a big swallow of hurt, exhaled a gale of discontent and said, 'One rupee a word is my fee, and the speeches are always three hundred words or more, never less. Though the speech is basically prepared on given points, I am constrained by no limits.' Seeing her making a face, I quickly added, 'Oh, I know, it isn't much by some standards. But, whatever money I make, is enough for survival.'

'I'm sorry. I really didn't mean to put you in a spot. What I really meant is that it's a seasonal job, which guarantees no steady income. Besides, one cannot be occupied throughout the year with that sort of petty assignment.'

'You're both right and wrong. But to explain it, I have to tell you all about the place I live in. Mention SHELTER to any cabby or autodriver and he would steer you straight to its doorstep, with a knowing smile. It's Delhi's most exclusive private lodge and a stable of diverse young aspirants, where the friendliness and intimacy of a home, are in abundance.

'They're all there. Writers, poets, painters, sculptors - all sorts of men of artistic originality. Unfortunately, none of us have a steady income. But we're never short of money. Joy and sorrow we share equally. We even exchange clothes and shoes, like brothers do at home. We're an oddly assorted lot, from different parts of India. Though each one of us is a beginner and quarrel often, we're tied by a steel bond as one lot, one bunch with one common aim, *creativity*.'

She listened intently as I talked myself out. Then, looking away for a moment, she turned back to me widening her eyes only to say, 'Great! All intellectuals!'

'And dreamers,' I quipped, and things were suddenly brighter and lighter between us.

Seven

For some time, a golden silence reigned within the coupe.

Her hand clasped in her lap, her eyes remote, her face in repose, she was poetically absorbed. It was this rare melodramatic pose, that had given her a completely feminine look. Physically she was near to me, though, mentally she was miles away.

Once it came to my mind to ask her what it was that absorbed her, so much, so quickly. But her maiden modesty and distinct dignity forbade me.

It wasn't more than five minutes afterwards, breaking that golden silence with a knock on the door, a voice announced:

'This is the time for the Littleman to come in, sir.'

Frowning, Dolly looked at me. Seeing the who-could-that-be look in each other's eyes, together we turned to the door.

The intruder, who called himself the Littleman and did not show up even after a minute of this funny announcement, kept us guessing.'

'Here I am,' at last the Littleman breezed in, smiling.

Although his smile was hundred per cent indigenous, it was marred by a front tooth half eaten away.

Looking at him we could now believe that the intruder was really a little man all of 4' 3", rumpled in white, cotton uniform, with a khaki cap and tennis shoes. He was a pleasantly, ugly little man, in his early forties, with a pitted bulbous nose. In his left hand he was holding a little order book, crammed with orders and a little pencil in his right. Stroking his little badge on the chest with the little pencil, he said:

'I'm no outsider, sir. 'I'm your most humble all-season-rail-host - the Littleman.'

We recognised him by his badge. He was the man from the railway dining car and now we looked at him with renewed interest, knowing what was coming.

'Lunch, madam?' he asked without preamble.

Dolly didn't make an answer to that. However, she was quick to ask me, 'Sanchu, aren't you hungry?'

'Very.'

'Me, too.'

'And the Littleman is here to take the orders.' Gliding a toothy smile, the diminutive rail host quickly transfixed his eyes on me.

'Two lunches, please.'

'Any special?' Dolly inquired.

'Yes, madam. There's chicken masala and fish fry.'

'You send both - two dishes each,' without asking for my assent, Dolly ordered extravagantly.

Not pleased with the liberties she permitted herself, I patiently waited for the Littleman to go.

'Thank you, madam.' So saying, as the Littleman bowed himself out, I gave Dolly a hard look.

But there was no indication of understanding in her face. Instead, a mischievous smile slowly spread around her lips.

'Why are you so serious, my friend?' she asked.

'Am I?' I countered, forcing a smile.

'I shouldn't have ordered those special dishes.'

It was part confession, part shame.

'It's all right,' I said, letting it go. 'Don't think about it.'

'I understand, Sanchu. Since you don't like your beautiful companion to be on the plump side, you didn't want her to order those rich, fattening, special dishes.'

Fascinated by this new piece of logic, I said, 'Only a fertile brain can invent such wonderful ideas.'

Seeing me laughing, she stuck out her tongue at me. Then, adopting an air of unconcern, gazed out of the window as if she did not care much.

A little jaded by her recurrent, erratic behaviour, I wished her to the devil and lay back, pillowing my head on my hands.

A good while went in silence, until she turned and caught me ogle at her smoothly shaped, provocative legs. She blushed. Awkwardly twitching her skirt downward, she said, by way of explanation:

'They give me freedom of movement. Besides, what else can I wear, on a hot, sticky day like this?'

It was really a hot day, unreasonable for October.

She was wearing a purple, midiskirt and a white, silk sleeveless blouse. I thought it was the latest fashion but she hinted at the weather.

Though her ready answer silenced me, my stunned eyes could not help looking at her face. Surprisingly enough, every time I looked at her face I saw a subtle difference. She was a beauty in every sense of the word.

'I think we're now beyond the stage of strangers, aren't we?'

'That goes without saying.'

'And yet you're looking at me a lot.' Her tone was severe but there was no anger.

'You see, I can't resist a pretty face.'

'That tells on one's moral unsoundness.'

'Don't make it sound worse than it is. After all, girl watching is second nature to most men. It's almost a law of nature.'

'That may be, but no girl these days, would tolerate a macho man.'

'If that is so, then give me one, good reason, why it has been going on, for ages.'

'Because girls have been ignoring; expecting men to reform themselves. Sad to say, men, till today, have not responded to reform in any desired number.'

'Suppose men refuse to be reformed, are women going to revolt against them?'

'Don't you think it's natural? Self-respect is as important to men as it is to us. It's a shame that men don't see this. However, if they don't come round faster, we've got ways to get around them.'

'You really are a queer sort of person.'

'Am I?'

'Yes, you are.'

'Very true. If you were not taking advantage of my being a woman.'

'That'll be the day, when anyone takes advantage of you.'

Shrugging aside my comment with disdain, smoothly she changed the track. 'Well, my friend, if it wasn't for the force of circumstances, I wouldn't have asked for the lift. But, by the time we reached Pune, I was bitten by the travel bug, the lure of adventure and all that.'

How was it that you didn't know earlier?'

'That was my folly, or you may say, my weakness.' Keeping her face expressionless, she continued, 'Seeing you all alone I volunteered to join the excursion. It's true, artistically we're not in the same beam, but basically, we both love travelling.'

'Indeed, a very nice thing to hear.'

Without paying any heed to my mumbling, she went on, 'Being travel companions, I thought, our requirement is mutual. But now, I feel differently.'

'Is that difference troubling you too much?'

'In that case you should go your own way.' Piqued by her annoyed tone, I rummaged out a ticket from my wallet and threw it on her face. 'Here, take it.'

'How could you abuse my weakness, Sanchu? That's not decent.' Then, on a hunch, she asked me a blunt question, 'Are you a Bengali by any chance?'

'One can't help being born a Bengali,' I replied evenly.

'That's the Bengali in you.'

'Exactly. That's the Bengali I am'

'But who told you you had to be rude?' Her voice was like a whiplash. Then, there came that sudden flash, that stab of knowledge which said, someone has to make this Bengali Babu know that its not *rosogolla* alone which sweetens one's tongue.

Wordless, as I was starting at her, the floodgates of all her accumulated anger, opened itself.

'You know, Sanchu, Bengalis are criticised everywhere for their rudeness.'

God, I thought, *that's why she asked me if I was a Bengali!*

'The trouble with you Bengalis is, that you're dictated by sentiments. You possess refinement, respect for tradition, thirst for knowledge, pride for ideals, sense of fairplay and justice, but your inherent rudeness, which is a by-product of sentiment, destroys the effect.'

'Being sentimental you tend to be straightforward. Do the Bengalis know what they are lacking today? Tact! In a world of conflicting moralities, tact is the logical substitute of straightforwardness.

'It's also a well known fact that you are a bunch of dreamers besotted with culture. You spend more time and money on it than you can afford. Idealism is a fine thing but you Bengalis have carried it too far. Now you cannot face a material fact when you meet one.'

I interrupted her tirade, 'Dolly, you're annoying me with insults.'

'Don't butt in, with objections. I detest interruptions.' Cutting me short, she went on bombarding me, with hard and stringent words. 'It is widely believed that Bengal played a leading part in the awakening of the Indian nation. The nation is grateful for their leadership.'

'Granted, Bengalis pioneered in all fields before Independence. But then was then, now is now. It is a pity that the Bengalis don't see this. The greatest irony is, that the unworthy descendants of the once great pioneers, love to bask in past glories.'

'What is left and over which they still have their mastery, is football. It means so much to the football crazy Bengalis, that they throng the playgrounds, deserting offices, schools and colleges. That's one place where they unite. Otherwise, they are divided about everything.'

It was the longest and hardest speech and the saddest to hear. I could not contain myself. I exploded into protest:

'For heaven's sake, Dolly, stop it.' There's a limit to tolerance. You have already gone too far. No further.'

'I knew you'd protest, because your pride has been wounded; but to be impatient is not etiquette.'

'Okay. Okay. Go ahead. I'm ready to swallow every insult.'

As before, she ploughed on, in her calm, condemning tone. 'The cultural arrogance and regional pride, make the Bengalis feel superior to those from other regions of the country. Today, of course, nobody cares for them. Even then, they puff up their chests. This is where their impracticability shows up, in its most embarrassing form. Worst of all, they seem to have no knowledge of what they have lost. Present day West Bengal, is the concrete example of Newtonian Physics—"What goes up, must come down".'

Her verbal blows, though they sound cynical to the ear, were as strong as they were accurate. I suddenly saw it all, with new eyes. Everything that Dolly emphasised upon, when summed up, read like an appeal to Bengalis to apprise how well their claims bear up, against the facts.

'Thank you, Dolly, for opening my eyes. Every word you said has a substratum of truth underlying it.'

She smiled and softened. Though her ultimate triumph eased her a bit, I noticed her anger was still not quenched.

'You must forgive us, Dolly,' I added solemnly, 'The Bengalis are a sentimental race.'

'I knew you'd agree. That makes a Bengali a Bengali.' Her face glowed with a confident, winning look. 'After all, Bengalis have a heart of gold. They are an understanding people. Only, at times, is their good sense marred by sheer sentimentality.'

Noticing how hurt I was, she wanted to say sorry, but her teenage ilk, slightly twisted it. 'I'm sure I've said my share of words which perhaps, I shouldn't have said.' Then, whirling round, she reached the overhead rack. Taking a few clothes out from her suitcase, a towel and soap from her travelling bag, she stomped off to the toilet.

Changing from the midi to a maxi, when she emerged, the lipstick was wiped off her mouth, her face clean and scrubbed, skin glowing and dark eyes searchingly alert. She walked back directly to her seat. Casually unconcerned with my presence, she dusted her seat and sat. While combing her hair, suddenly she remembered to ask.

'Sanchu, does travel really broaden the mind?'

The suddenness of the question took me by surprise.

'Whether or not, you shouldn't have taken the risk of travelling with a stranger.'

'Would you believe, being adventurous, I'm prone to risk?'

'To risk everything to give oneself some adventure is utterly suicidal.'

'Try telling that to any girl today and she would say, your social views haven't changed.'

'I think she'd still be wrong to say that.'

'Don't you worry. Nobody's going to blame you for eloping,' she giggled wickedly.

'That's sheer nonsense!' I said, adding with some bitterness. 'You women seem to have dirty minds.'

'Dear man of our generation, don't despair. God Almighty made women to match men.' She said, smiling sarcastically. 'We women, therefore, urge our counterpart, the so-called superior menfolk, to get rid of the fooling notions that women are this, women are that, etcetera, etcetera.'

'Dolly, don't twist words to suit your convenience.'

Raising a silencing palm to forestall my objections, she prattled on, her mouth going faster than the Japanese bullet train. 'Tell me what's the difference between a boy and a girl, in these fast moving, hi-tech times of ours? You can't tell one, from the other. In similar, faded jeans and grubby T-shirts, slacks and sandals, boots and beliefs, you'll find girls frequenting the cinemas and theatres, parks and beaches. Like boys, these present-day, carefree, modern girls freely drink, dance and smoke, in pubs and clubs, at dinners and parties. They have even changed the style of walk, from female to male, to match men.'

'In short, modern girls have this idiotic idea that to be men's equal, to get a job and find a place in the 'male' world, not only must they put aside everything that is called 'feminine', but also their mystiques. Instead of taking the best traits, like assertiveness, they are only trying to look more, like men. And that's where they are lacking. Tell me, can a woman become a man by getting into man's clothing and changing her walking style?'

The question massacred her vanity.

When there was no reply to my question, even after several seconds, I counselled,

'First and foremost, a modern, teenage girl should know what is modernity. Also, she herself should set a self-regulating code of her own limitations.'

This irked Dolly. 'Why do men have the tendency to advise women? Disgusting! More so, when it is unsolicited.'

'It's sheer vanity. Although Mother Nature has endowed women with endurance, tolerance, kindness and grace, their inherent vanity can turn the sweet image sour, just as acidity can cause milk to curdle. Need I say more, stupid girl?'

'So who the hell are you? My mentor? My Guru? Ha! Advising me like I was born yesterday!'

'No passport. No visiting card. No identity card to prove who I am. Nor can I hide what I am. I, therefore, have no choice but to agree to whatever you take me for. Still, I'll not make any secret of my views, that a disturbing proportion of urban, teenage girls, with a come-hither look, are a common sight these days. It is this decadent lifestyle that is damaging the pleasure of their being women and, ultimately, loosing the respect and dignity of womanhood.'

'Shut your big mouth. Now it's getting on my nerves. Just one word more and your ass will be kicked.'

Her offensive utterance battered me into silence.

At that moment I heard,

'Banish anger, satisfy hunger.' It was Littleman's jolly voice calling for an immediate cease-fire.

Next was his delightful entry, with the gust of an instinctive clown, followed by two waiters, carrying heaped plates.

With the arrival of our lunches, the heated argument stopped, bringing a temporary armistice.

Dolly smiled smugly, winked, snapped the rubber band on to her hair and tried to look demure. Left with no choice, I winked back and stayed calm.

No sooner had lunch been served and the Littleman had backed away with the waiters, Dolly started spooning her tomato soup.

'Mmmmm! The tomato soup isn't bad, Sanchu and I always enjoy thick soup.'

Looking at the hungry teenager's glowing face, my appetite evaporated.

'You haven't touched your soup Anything wrong?' asked Dolly.

'My problem is… I'm allergic to tomato,' I bluffed.

That gave my greedy companion instant access to my bowl of soup. With a faint shrug of my shoulders, I ticked off her schoolgirl appetite and concentrated on the meal.

For some time, we ate in a contended silence. Then, for no reason, I took a peek at my companion.

Watching her tasting the masala chicken, reflecting upon its flavour and then biting into a chicken leg and licking her fingers, murmuring ecstatically to herself, I thought that she was an addict to good food.

'Aahaa! How is this masala chicken, Sanchu?' The 'eat more - worry less' girl, asked between mouthfuls.

'Fine,' I said, without tasting it.

'And this side dish of fried, potato slices, to go with the fish fry?' Spraying pepper and salt, she scooped a forkful and tossed it into her mouth.

While I was still nibbling at the fish fry, Dolly, stuffed to the gills, pushed her plate aside, with a satisfied sigh, giving the impression of a good eater. Then, moving closer to the window, she looked out impassively.

Abandoned, I hurried through the meal. There was one thought, however, which rankled me: *How to get even with this rich, pampered girl.*

And now, with the meal over, I lit a cigarette. Softened somewhat, which was the effect of the good meal, my eyes were drawn to the extraordinary teenager who, by then, had her nose buried in a book.

For the first time all day, I was tempted to know more about her fiancé, the young millionaire. But she was being very secretive and sensitive about her personal matters. What would her reactions be, if asked, was what was worrying me.' However, after a few contemplative puffs, I took a chance to talk her into it.

'Dolly, I was wondering about what you were saying before about the young millionaire.'

Without marking the page, Dolly closed her book and turned to me.

'What made you wonder?'

'Only this that you could have married the young millionaire and set out for your honeymoon to places like Darjeeling, Nainital, Ooty... rather than come with me, to an old city in ruins.'

'Indisputably you're right. But I don't ever want to marry a young millionaire.'

'Why then, do you choose to remain engaged to him?'

'Can't you see, that way, I'm safe for the time being? Grandma won't worry me and my parents would not bother her.'

'But that's dishonest.'

'Surely not.' She shook her head defiantly. Then a sly grin lighted her face. 'When you life is in danger, everything is fair.'

'The reason is not very sound, is it?'

'If you like, I'll explain about the young millionaires.'

'Do go on.'

'What I mean to say is that young millionaires have a lot of vices. Those vices are the gift of their ancestors. Along with hereditary wealth, they inherit the vices, also.'

'It cannot be an infallible rule.'

She overlooked my objection, with a queer little smile.

'Usually young millionaires are like that. It is a well known fact that those who lead an easy life are not strong.'

Her reply was irrefutable.

Then the waiters returned and were busily removing empty plates and used stainless steel wares. I turned my head to see what Dolly was doing. I found her sleeping, drawing the bedclothes up, over her shoulders.

There was grace and mystery in her attitude, as if she were a symbol of something. If I were a painter I would have painted her in that attitude and captioned the picture, 'A Lonely Rebel'.

A single glance at Dolly would tell a man that literally, the name perfectly matched her identity.

Seeking justification, I continued to look at her covertly, and indeed, the name, A Lonely Rebel, fitted Dolly like hand and glove.

Pleased with myself, I lit another cigarette, my eyes still fastened on the sleeping beauty. Suddenly I realised that she was a rare jewel, a prize to be won. My indiscreet sense of owning her, was rapidly heightened and I imagined her in my arms, being kissed by me.

That very moment she stirred.

Not to be caught, quickly pulling away my eyes from her, I puffed steadily on my cigarette, as though I found salvation in it.

But she did not open her eyes, she curled up in her sleep, turned her back to me and started snoring.

When sleeping soundly, it is natural to snore, if your belly is full. What is natural is never vulgar.

The train had picked up speed after a brief halt. The perpetual clatter of the wheels, surprisingly, sounded much like Dolly's picture's name, 'A Lonely Rebel', as it sped on and on.

Eight

WHEN IN MANDU STAY AT HAPPY HOME. A HOME AWAY FROM HOME WITH ALL MODERN AMENITIES.

The first thing that caught my eyes was the poster, in extra-bold, shining letters, as we came out of the Mhow Railway Station. All the while, I was worrying about a place to stay; but now longer; once my mind was made up, to patronise the Happy Home.

Immediately after light refreshments, we started off, from the shadow into the sun, in a taxi, for Mandu. Despite the apparent dangers on that bone shaking potholed road, winding through rocky gorges and hills, the cabby delivered us to Happy Home, by the day's end.

Happy home was a huge, century-old bungalow, with a rose garden. The place had all the pretensions to grandeur that such old places usually have. It boasted homely comforts and other amenities. But a hotel was a hotel, a profit-making place, no matter how hard one tried to make it look like a home. Expecting someone from the hotel would come to pick up our luggage, we lingered on, outside the gate, chatting.

Suddenly, there was a minor uproar. Behind us, a private bus, packed with students, none older than sixteen pulled up. As they tumbled out, I heard many voices passing remarks, targeting us.

'Arrey Anil, jori kem laage chey tane? (What do you make of the couple, Anil?)' Said one, twinkling at another with secret amusement.

'Mane to aa khoti jori laage cheey. (I think they are a spurious pair),' Anil replied, eyeing us with suspicion.

'Arrey jaa jaa! (Go, man go)' a girl countered the boy's impertinent remarks. *'Kala chashma peherine baddu kaluj dekhai cheey.* (he, who wears dark glasses, sees everything dark).'

The boy pulled off his sunglasses, then challenged: *'Naina, aa vaat par sau-sau ni laagi sharat.* (Naina, let us bet a hundred bucks).'

Naina, the leader of the party, before accepting the bet, exchanged fleeting glances with the other girls, for consent. When everyone nodded agreement she felt a thrill of pride and doubled the bet money.

Ba-sau. (Two hundred).'

'*Laagi.* (Taken)' The boys promptly welcomed it.

Judging us to be non-Gujratis they were, I deduced, so loud-mouthed about us. Now quickly grabbing our luggage, we went through the garden, then up the steps, into the reception hall.

'Welcome to Happy Home.' The white uniformed receptionist behind the desk, smiled at Dolly. She indicated a grey, leather-bound register. 'If you please,' she said. 'It's a rule of the Happy Home that all tourists have to check in.'

A frown of annoyance crossed Dolly's face, while she was registering. Thereupon, the Gujrati boys and girls came in and congregated around us.

Dolly had just signed. The receptionist, handing a key to her, said, 'Room sixteen is a few doors down the corridor.'

In the meantime, the leader of the party had taken the register from Dolly's hand and the fun started.

'Hey, I've won the bet.'

'What does the entry read?' demanded the stocky boy.

'Well...'

The leader's chin lifted a little. Holding the grey book, she fumbled for words.

From the way she was fumbling, there seemed something fishy going on.

'Naina!' the boys decried.

'Don't bark!'

The leader's harshest remark sparked protests.

Not heeding them, Naina volunteered herself in listing her inmates in the hotel register.

'You don't get the bet money if you don't read it out loud and clear,' warned the stocky boy.

'I don't care,' Naina snapped back, without a feeling of loss.

'But we do,' retorting sharply, the stocky boy bulled his way through the crowd of tourists to the counter, snatched the register from the leader's hand and loudly read out: 'Husband and wife.'

'No life without wife,' the sensation monger of the lot blurted out the choicest phrase.

The Happy Home resounded to a roar of 'Yeah-yeah-yeah!

Every head strained for a look at us and the atmosphere at the Happy Home reception hall, was charged with terrifying excitement.

We, merely trying to stem the mad situation, bowed ceremoniously to the frolickers.

The climax came when the hotel owner himself, joined the fun. 'Let's give the honeymooning couple a loud, hearty cheer!'

Instantly, the 'Yeah-yeah-yeah' faded, to be replaced by 'Hear-hear'.

We gave them a happy smile, in return.

Now that our false connubiality was accepted as real, we felt relieved and made for room sixteen, which was on the ground floor of the west wing, with a fine view of the rose garden.

Reaching our room, I began to suspect Dolly of being a boy-trap. In fact, the doubt had been gnawing me inwardly, for some time, but it remained there for want of an outlet. Unable to keep it within any longer, I gave it an opening as she came out of the bathroom, looking pleasant in an evening gown, with a gay, tra-la-la on her lips.

'It's just not true.'

'What is just not true?'

'Our relationship you mentioned in the hotel register. I suppose you have some explanation.'

'Oh,' breaking into an enigmatic smile, she asked coyly, 'am I not worth it?'

'Indeed, Miss Worth. You're worth a good deal more. Unfortunately, this staunch bachelor has no plans of settling down.'

'I've no plans for that, either. This deliberate lie which I have written in the register is for our safety's sake, without any motive.'

'I'm afraid I do not share a woman's privilege.' For a moment, some of the glow left Dolly's face. I continued, 'You know the hotel register will hold our names as husband and wife, for all time.'

'How very comforting to know that from you, of all people,' she said, in a pained voice. I never thought my honest intention would be misinterpreted by you, to humiliate me!'

'Possibly I've hurt you.'

'Possibly?' She shot me a look both wary and forbidding. 'Whenever I make an attempt to create a friendly relationship, you spoil it by picking up a quarrel. Why? Why? Why?'

'Because I am not quite used to such lies.'

'Oh God!' She wailed, pounding her temples. 'Why did I come into contact with this *Yudhishthira!*'

'Quit repenting,' I told her. 'You go your way, I go mine. The matter ends.'

'No. It doesn't end there.' Crying bitterly, she flew at me. Her eyes emitting fire, her clenched fists pummelling at my chest. 'No, no, no. It doesn't end there.'

I caught her wrists and held her still. Only for a moment she looked at me levelly, then she slumped against me, weeping.

Touched by her tears, I took her into my arms. She held on to me tightly and began to cry.

'I'm sorry. Very, very sorry.'

'I feel such a fool,' she said frostily.

'I'm sorry you feel this way, but I was only joking.'

'You don't have to pacify me.' She pulled herself free and reached for her travelling bag and suitcase. Then, turning in indignation, she gave me a stabbing glance of anger. 'From the beginning, you were all the time fighting, arguing and bickering as if you had a license to hurt. I can't take it anymore. I'm leaving this room right now.'

In that hot moment I stood there rooted, watching her go, gripped by despair.

At the door she halted, then, veering round she asked, 'You said you were joking. Were you?'

'Yes, if you believe me.'

Dolly, mild yet wild, now sad, now glad, was a girl of many moods. Dropping her suitcase and travelling bag on the floor, she quickly brushed the tears from her eyes, wore a smile on her face and with her arms outstretched, said, 'Touch me and say.'

Going a few steps forward, I held her proffered hands with affection and whispered assurances.

'Swear?'

'Swear?'

Thus, peace dawned upon us, after a rancorous quarrel, like a perfume after rancid filth.

Absurdly, unexpectedly, she flung her arms around me, a romantic product of a girlish imagination.

Her body pressed against me and the sense of contact was electric. The feeling of need and want that we had for each other, was felt for the first time, at that exciting moment. It was not an illusion, but genuinely real and something of substance.

'What an emotional little thing you are!' I tweaked her nose. 'You know I'm getting to like you.'

'Sanchu darling, you're the sweetest!' My partner-in-travel, prompted by cupidity, wrapped her arms widely around me and pulled me close, compelling me to bend over her.

Two faces within breathing distance; no way could we resist from doing the craziest things. At this juncture, the door swung open and the Gujrati girl sailed in, shattering the mood of the moment.

Extricating myself guiltily, I managed to say, 'Hi-girls! But they made a quick right about-turn, blushing.

By then, Dolly had recovered her composure. 'What is it girls?' She called after the shy collegians. 'Is there anything we can do for you?'

They stopped. With their feet glued to the floor, eyes downcast, they stayed just as they were, tongue-tied.

To save them from awkwardness, I said encouragingly, 'You girls don't hesitate. My wife is exceedingly good. Especially, when it comes to sheltering damsels in distress, she has no equal.

Conquering shyness, the head girl now turned on her heels, advanced slowly towards Dolly and whispered into her ear: '*Didi*, our Professor Saab hasn't arrived so far.'

'So, my dears?' Dolly was smiling.

'We're afraid some boys may take advantage of his absence.'

'Courage, girls.'

'No *Didi*, one of the boys is dangerously naughty.'

Dolly clicked her tongue disapprovingly. 'Usually naughty boys are not dangerous.'

'But *Didi*, he is altogether a different type.'

'Well, if he blows hot, you blow cold,' Dolly advised them, with sisterly candour.

'Not with the obnoxious one.'

'Is he that bad?'

'Worse.'

After pouring out their troubles on Dolly's neck, they waited hopefully.

Dolly pondered this, for a grave moment. 'Well, I do understand your position.'

'We want you to help us, *Didi*.'

'Tell me, girls what help do you expect of me?'

'Just shelter us in your room tonight.'

It was a woman calling out to another woman, on the subject which inevitably binds the female race, whatever their stratum of life, whatever their creed, colour, nationality or clothes.

She did some quick thinking. 'Girls, if you all think it absolutely necessary, you're welcome.' Then, turning to me with her most winning grin, she appealed, 'They've come to spend the night with me, dear.'

'And I should stay out! Is that what you mean, darling?'

'Honestly dear, you're very good at mind-reading.'

I, pretending to be hurt, said, 'Yes, darling, even to you I'm now an unwanted intruder, an unloved stranger.'

'Why do you say that, my love? Don't we see enough of each other all day?' Dolly reasoned, masking it, in sweet politeness.

'We do see enough of each other all day. But they don't know what the night means to the newly weds. Fancy you choosing otherwise.'

'Sorry, dear,' Dolly said, with a wifely smile, 'but it seems unavoidable.'

At this point, one of the girls showed up with a bedsheet and pillow, rolled in a blanket.

Dolly was actually waiting for the package. Now, tucking it under my arm, she waived me out. 'Be off! You've no business here, tonight.'

'The waste of such a beautiful night. You shall regret this all your life,' I fired the last warning shot and trotted off.

Peals of feminine laughter echoed throughout the Happy Home, to crown my gay joke.

Nine

Reaching the portico, I thanked the girls mutely for their timely intervention, thus saving both Dolly and me, from the unknown awkwardness of sleeping in the same bed with the false title of husband and wife.

Standing there, poised with relief, I heard the leader praising my acting wife.

'We're thankful and blessed beyond measure, to find a *Didi* like you.'

'No sleep tonight, my sweeties,' Dolly told them, disregarding the praise.

'What shall we do then? Swat mosquitoes?' They asked. But Dolly did not share the banal joke. Her reply, 'One minute,' set them all agog.

In the middle of this waiting silence I wanted a cigarette very badly. I slapped my pockets but remembering where I had left the packet, I started back for the room. Though the atmosphere of the room was in low-key now, the jingle of bangles, perfume and giggles, had converted it into a ladies parlour. Not wanting to intrude, I hesitated at the door.

Dolly, bent over the open attaché case before her, was groping for something. Presently, she swung round in a single movement, holding aloft a pack of cards like a victory banner.

'Girls,' Dolly called out loudly, throwing the pack on the bed, 'we will play bridge.'

'Wonderful!' The girls squealed with joy, clapping.

Dolly smiled broadly at their renewed compliments.

Clamouring, they now moved to the bed and sat down in a circle. The fairest girl shuffled the deck twice and began distributing, with the amazing rapidity of an expert.

By the time Dolly joined them with a sheet of paper and pencil, the deal was over. Before taking her place, she felt someone was standing at the door. On her face a surge of irrational rage came and went, when she saw me.

'Oh heavens, do you have to pry into our room?' With hands on her hips, she commanded severely, 'Stay out. Your sex doesn't entitle you to join women.'

I smiled but made no move. 'I want my cigarette, left on the shelf.'

'You made it this far,' she rasped, 'you may as well come in and take it yourself.'

Keeping calm and casual, I crossed the room to the shelf and picked up the pack of Charms. Whistling softly as I walked back to the door, one of the girls remarked in a timid voice:

'Poor hubby! Two-heads-on-one-pillow is not for him tonight.'

And the whole lot giggled except the pigtailed, impish girl, with a curl right in the middle of her forehead, who jolted everybody, by heightening the sexiest joke, with a wisecrack beyond her years.

'It is far worse for *Didi*. No arm shall slither past her breast or thighs tonight.'

Dumbfounded, for several awkward seconds, nobody spoke. And then, suddenly, they were laughing, great wondrous whoops of laughter.

But, in that all-girl, friendly atmosphere, Dolly's high-pitched laughter outrang all the others. She laughed so hard her stomach ached and tears spilled from her eyes.

Back in the portico as I lit a cigarette, someone in the room asked: 'Whose call?'

'Naina's call,' replied a good looking girl, typically Gujrati, with eyes which were sandy brown and black hair, parted in the middle, plaited and worn in coils over both ears.

'Two hearts,' Called Naina in a luscious voice, then looked coquettishly at Dolly and added, 'beating as one, now stopped on separation.'

'Naughty!' said Dolly, lowering her lashes, and the girls broke into a sudden ripple of laughter.

In all their hundred years, the rooms of hotel Happy Home hadn't heard so much laughter. The stone walls that wept usually, with the damp from the river Narmada, glistened now with laughter. Wafting along the corridors, the ripples entered the rooms and downed the gentle snores of the sleeping tourists.

When laughter subsided, Dolly called: 'Two spades.'

'Two no-trump.'

'Pass.'

Still puffing, I was amusing myself with their amateurish bridge calls.

'Three spades.'

'Double.'

'Three no-trump.'

The boys were now returning from their night rambles, their voices floating in, loud and clear. To save them from the peril of my presence, I made myself as comfortable as I could, on a creaky, wooden bench and tried to catch a few winks of sleep.

They came. They changed. They whispered. They argued. They laughed. They took their own time to switch off the lights before going to bed.

Students are students, anytime and anywhere. Religion, region or caste, makes no difference. Born gentle, nourished in hope, these naïve teenagers are often politicised by the self-seeking, political Gurus, ultimately leading them to prematurely ruined lives. Somehow, banishing the erratic thoughts when I went to sleep, I dreamed.

In my dream I dredged up a pleasant chapter of Manu's history:

... On a clear, moonlit night, on the green banks of the Narmada everything in the vicinity was peacefully quiet, except for the rippling sound of its swiftly flowing waters.

Suddenly, the 'quiet' was broken by a haunting melody, a voice so lilting, that the rippling river gentled its flow.

Rupmati, the legendary singer of Mandu, was singing the praises of Narmada, of which she was a humble devotee.

Baz Bahadur, the poet Sultan of Mandu, sitting on the greens under a tree, only a few yards from the huge boulder that lay by the riverbank, on which Rupmati stood, was deeply engrossed, composing poems. Incidentally, it was one of the chosen places for his imaginative writing. Distracted, he looked up and easily spotted Rupmati, but she did not seem to notice him.

In the midst of nature's splendour, she was gazing ecstatically at her reflection in the swirling waters. God knows what crossed her mind and she lifted her diaphanous veil. Baz Bahadur caught his breath in disbelief. She was the most beautiful woman he had ever laid eyes on. For him it was a moment of sheer euphoria.

'What an apparition!' The words emanating from the heart, in genuine appreciation, sent him quickly behind the tree, lest his presence scare her.

Although it was her domain, having exclusive command over everything, she still wasn't aware of the invading intruder. For her, a night dip in the holy river, was a religious ritual. At first she removed the ornaments, then slipped off her clothes, without any consternation.

Rupmati, nude now, her alabaster skin glowed in the silvery moonlight. She paused for a moment, sucking in her breath, then dived into the shimmering river. Sleekly, smoothly, cutting the water like a scythe, she was cruising against the tide, concentrating on speed, as if she had done it every night, for years.

After successfully crossing the river twice, she swam back to the boulder, and then, like a dolphin, leapt out of the water, right on the top. Drenched with divinity, she now lay herself down, gasping for air. Being accustomed to such boundless freedom, she was as slow as she was careless, in reaching for the clothes.

Long afterwards, rested and dressed, when she was ready to go, with every piece of ornament back in place, the Sultan's self-control betrayed him and he emerged from behind the tree.

Frightened, she drew the veil. But the next moment, inhaling courage, she swivelled round, to face him.

'Who're you?' She challenged, her face looking as hard as a face stamped on a coin.

'Before I answer you, tell me are you real or a mirage?'

'It seems you don't know the consequences of such shameless intrusion upon the privacy of a woman.'

'What will be, will be! Please tell whether you are real or a mirage?'

'I'm as real as you. And you?'

'Sultan Baz Bahadur.'

Taken aback by his precise response, she nearly fainted. 'Ma Narmada, save me!' she prayed silently, turning on her heels.

Suddenly her feet sped of their own accord, her *bindi* glowed and illumined her path, her anklets flashed, her *pochas* and bangles quivered with fear and her *jhoomkas* and *nathni* oscillated to her hurrying trend, ringing danger.

'You spoiled everything,' the poet Sultan blamed himself and stood still, staring after Rupmati's retreating figure.

'Wake up, Sanchu!' Dolly's repetitive calls jerked me out of my dream. Drowsily, I babbled a few curses and soon fell into a dreamless sleep.

Ten

Sometime later.

Awakened by dawn's chorus, when the sun was barely up and the air was cool and quiet, I found the hotel humming with excitement.

'Good morning, Professor Saab,' the boys and girls chimed together.

Professor Saab! Taken aback, I rubbed my eyes and looked intently at the lovely face, for a moment longer.

Dolly, totally unrecognisable, clad in a *sari*, her hair let loose, a *bindi* on her forehead, greeted me with a 'Hi'. The momentary flicker of her right eye, supported by a persuasive smile, further carried me away, leaving me with no choice but to accept this new role. And then, the writer-turned-professor switched his attention to the impatient students.

'Good morning, Ladies and Gentlemen. Gosh! Are all of you ready?'

'It is already six, sir.' One of the girls held her wristwatch under my nose.

'Give me five minutes and I'll be with you,' I assured them and made a dash for the room.

When we reached the historic sight, Dolly made a surprise announcement:

'Attention, Baroda students! Professor Sanchu will give a short speech about the place.'

The announcement was loudly applauded.

Tired of Dolly's propensity to say the wrong thing at the wrong time, I shot her a stony look. But, the silent rebuke in my eyes, made no impact.

Is she playing the fool with me or trying to humiliate me? The search for the answer in my mind was still on, when she spoke in a whispered voice: 'This is your opportunity to prove how good a history professor you are.'

'I need no opportunity for anything.'

'But I've made the announcement mentioning your name.'

'Sorry. I can't carry out the mandate.'

'Be nice, please. It looks silly to delay further.'

'Tricky girl, don't expect me to be nice, after pushing me to the wall.'

That chilled her to the bone.

'Sanchu, please!' She implored, grabbing my hand. 'It's time you told the students about Mandu.'

Dolly was worried that the students, who were quiet till then, would cease to be so, if the announced speech was not forthcoming. Being a fair-minded man, I didn't want to prolong it further.

'Okay, let me try.'

Now, marvelling at the ardent students in front of me, history resurrected itself.

'This is Mandu, a ghost town, slumbering among the forts, palaces, tombs, havelis and more, spread over some twenty-five miles. What is now in ruins was built and fashioned by the hands of man. It has no less than seventy-five remarkable monuments, set among reflecting lakes and ponds.

'In the days of *Vikramaditya*, Mandu is said to have been a stronghold of the shepherd kings. From the tenth to thirteenth centuries, it was ruled by the Paramara kings of Malwa. But little remains of ancient Hindu Mandu, beyond traces of its fortification and the manes who dwell in scared springs and tanks.

'In 1304, General Ain-ul-Mulk, under orders from Sultan Ala-ud-din-Khilji of Delhi, fell upon king Malik Deo. Mandu, thus, passed under the sovereignty of Delhi. But the security offered by this unique site, tempted its governors to throw off their allegiance to the Sultanate and assume royal powers. This Jama Masjid, where we are standing now, and Hashang Shah's tomb are spots pulsating with silent emotions.

'Architecture is history written in stone. These buildings are the finest examples of Afghan architecture in India and they reveal to us clearly, the lives of the Sultans, their habits, their culture, their character and their thought.' Dishing out a slice of history, when I looked round at Dolly, I found a very deep appreciation hiding behind her mischievous eyes.

Thus entrenching myself as an expert history professor, I said rather pompously, 'Though my grasp of history is a bit shaky, I hope you aren't disappointed.'

'Not at all. Rather, it turned out so well, that given half a chance, you might prove yourself a distinguished historian.'

'No use glorifying a fake. And that is the plain truth…'

'By the way,' suddenly lowering her voice to a confidential whisper, she asked, 'was the speech a prepared one?'

'No.'

'How did you manage then?'

'Purely accidental. Recently, I happened to read all about Mandu, in a historical journal.'

'Lucky guy,' she repressed a smile upon the sly. 'Even then you deserve a cheer.'

'That's very inspiring indeed!' I laughed at Dolly's sudden shift, from mockery to flattery.

Checkmated, she stayed dumb..

Now when I was pleased with myself for defeating Dolly in her fooling game, something happened within the students and a row developed. I was forced to turn my attention to the overexcited students, yelling at each other.

'Hey boys, surely there must be a better way of kicking up a row.'

'Sorry sir, if we've disturbed you,' they replied, with a touch of mischief.

'Hardly. I prefer boisterous youngsters to dull goody-goodies.'

No reprimand but praise. That lifted the attention seekers' spirits high. Galloping, they came and encircled me. As in a mad house, everybody spoke at once. 'Sir! Sir!...'

'Stop fussing,' I censured.

In less than a second, there was complete silence.

'I think Naina, senior among you, should tell me about the tantrums,' I offered.

Naina looked around at them, as they stared silently at each other.

'Don't be shy,' I encouraged, adding, 'Speak out, whatever it is.'

Finally Naina spoke. 'Sir, a humble request...'

'Autograph?'

Before she could answer the others sang out. 'No, Sir! We want to be photographed with you.'

'Let me warn you, I am not photogenic.'

For almost two minutes, Dolly had been keeping a low profile. Eventually, she insinuated herself back into the conversation.

'It does not matter if one is not photogenic in a group of photogenic girls and boys.'

'*Didi* is right,' said Naina excitedly.

'*Didi* is absolutely right,' Naina's gang repeated in unison.

Not very long after, to pose for a group photo, we had positioned ourselves in front of the Hindole Mahal, the palace whose battered walls and buttresses created the illusion of the swinging building, which had given it, its name. When the camera was about to click, a lone, Siberian, white crane, looking for breakfast, uttered a harsh cry, from a rock, on the lake nearby, compelling us to shift our gaze to this non-resident Indian. Soon afterwards, exacting the reason, as our eyes returned to the camera, the shutter clicked.

Breaking up noisily, we took the marble path that led to the massive front door, with engravings. It was in the centre of a wide, colonnaded terrace, which appeared to surround the whole lower floor of the palace.

A squadron of bats flickered as we entered.

'At one time this was the abode of sultans and begums. Now, the only residents are lizards and bats. 'Shahiabad Mandu' is no longer a city of joy, but a city of distress.'

My remarks set the strings of sorrow, in the young hearts, vibrating. They followed me silently. At the terrace, still sad, they stood behind me, gazing upon the panorama of jungle, lake, tanks and mountains. Pointing to the Reva Tank, I delivered another piece of lecture, to melt the cold sadness that had gripped them.

'That's Reva Tank, constructed in fulfilment of Rupmati's wish. Over the centuries, it has turned into a place of pilgrimage for the Hindus, while still, to this day, it's the main source of water for the local people. On the lofty crest of the hill beyond the palace of Baz Bahadur, Rupmati's arched pavilion is languishing in silence. There she would come everyday, it is said, and gaze down dreamily at the sacred, silvery thread of the Narmada.'

'Who was Rupmati, sir?' The quietest boy of the lot abruptly questioned.

'A common, shepherd girl, who was destined to be a queen. Legend has it that during the first half of the sixteenth century, the great romance of Rupmati with Baz Bahadur, the last of the independent Sultan of Malwa, was born, while she was bathing in the Narmada.

'Baz Bahadur was attracted by the sweet voice of the beautiful Hindu singer, Rupmati, but was unable to persuade her to leave the banks of the Narmada, of which she was a devotee, till he had agreed to construct a tank and feed it with Narmada's waters. They then returned together to Mandu, where Rupmati became the melody and love of his life. The love of Rupmati and Baz Bahadur became a favourite theme of songs, poetry and painting. As fate would have it, Baz Bahadur proved to be valiant only in song. He fled, when Akbar's general, Adham Khan, attacked Mandu, abandoning Rupmati, who ended her life by taking poison.'

Quoting lines from history's pages as I ended my lecture, a romantic melody, one of Baz Bahadur and Rupmati's love songs sung till date, in Malwa, came floating to our ears, from the flute of a herder.

At the pleasant sound, blooming lotuses on the sun-blessed water of the Munj Talao, shivered; a passing, shy village belle, attired in her ancestral style, stood confused for a fraction of a minute and again moved on, swinging her *dupatta* in the air; bent heads of grazing cows jerked up and the tiny bells tied round their necks tinkled gently. For moments their eyes swung about before resting on the herder playing the flute sitting on the fork of the lone *sisham* tree.

A bevy of milkmaids carrying empty brass pots, laughingly swinging their way home, suddenly stood still on the *katchcha* pathway, by the bank of the lake. The round, high breasted women, each tapered to a handspan waist, swelling and curving voluptuously to the hips, immortalised in our sculptures, captured centuries ago in stone, seemed to be alive, in those reflections of the milkmaids, under the crystal water of the Munj Talao.

The moment they came to know of our presence, life returned electrically to those alluring figures. Walking with natural grace, they went away giggling.

Eleven

Spending some memorable hours in the historical surroundings of Mandu, we returned to the Happy Home before dark.

The colourful girls and cheerful boys of the Baroda College, swarmed in, laughing and giggling, only to stop dead, near the steps of the main hall.

'Quiet!' The stocky boy alerted his classmates, 'Professor Dave.'

Their history professor, Mr Dave, fat and flabby, round and chubby, seated with his back to the wall, was reading a newspaper.

Several moments passed. The silence grew heavier with every passing moment.

The newspaper had hidden the professor's face, preventing the shifting eyes from discerning his mood. He kept on his pretence of reading the newspaper. Then suddenly, throwing it down he looked up.

'Why, if it isn't my lot! What do you mean going off like that?'

Everyone tensed, but they digested this in silence.

For a few seconds, the professor studied their downcast heads.

The dead silence indicated their genuine repentance.

'Crazy idiots!' he muttered. Then he spoke aloud, but this time good humouredly, to minimise the tension. 'Sorry, it's all my fault, I missed the bus.'

'But we didn't miss any lecture, sir,' cried the boy and girls together.

With a flicker of a smile on his lips, Mr Dave comfortably settled himself back in the chair.

Encouraged by his changing mood, Naina made the intros.

'Sir, please meet professor Sanchu from Delhi…'

'Hey there! I'm professor Dave.'

Before Mr Dave was able to get out of the chair, I reached him and put out my hand.

'A pleasure, Mr Sanchu.' We shook hands.

'We had a nice time with Mr and Mrs Sanchu, who kindly showed us around Mandu and before asking what we were seeing or where we were standing, briefed us on the related historical facts.' Naina's exasperated tones convinced Mr Dave.

Even so, Professor Dave wanted to know if they had learnt all that is essential to know about Mandu and a chorus of 'Yes sir', answered him.

'For his kind act, I find it difficult to express my gratitude…'

While Professor Dave's voice searched for suitable words of praise, Dolly cried petulantly, 'Don't you worry about that, Mr Dave. My husband is not very keen on compliments. A simple 'Thank you' will do.'

'Why are you taking it the wrong way, Mr Sanchu? A compliment is usually a lie, but gratitude is the homage of the heart.'

'No offence meant.' I interjected in a bid to reverse the surprising turn in the conversation. 'I only did what a lot of other people had done before. I'm nothing special… I deserve neither praise nor compliments. But, the one thing that I can assure you is we both had a lovely day in the company of the best and the brightest students.'

'That's very assuring, Mr Sanchu. I respect your integrity. Ostensibly, you're the right man, in the right place, at the right time. All along I was worrying about this trip, but you've eased my problem.'

'Problem? The students, you mean?'

'Oh no! Emphatically negating it, professor Dave said, 'My charming figure is my biggest problem.' And in the same breath he went on to say, 'Look at this young herd, slim and trim, each weighing less than 60 kilos, just half my weight. Tell me how is it possible for this 'fatso' to go round places, with these fast-moving swifts?'

An outburst of laughter rippled through the hall.

'Silence!' The professorial voice brought them all back to order immediately. Pleased with his lot, Mr Dave's eyes beamed behind the black-rimmed glasses. 'There is a general impression that the main part of history education is the acquisition of facts and seeing historical remains, only. But it's not true. They just stimulate one's historical curiosity.' Thus giving the impression of superiority his eyes swept... particularly over our faces.

The unwanted criticism came as a rude shock. Feeling offended Dolly and I exchanged quick glances. Indirectly, Professor Dave's uncalled for remark, was tantamount to letting me down.

Although the students were quite familiar with his witticism, with each passing moment their spirits sank lower, wondering what was coming. But their wonder did increase further, when the august professor deliberately asked a funny question.

'Has anyone of you ever tried to trace the origin of the seven letter word "history"?'

The odd question was greeted with blank stares. But the complacent smile on the professor's face proclaimed that only he knew the answer. Several moments of silence followed, before we heard him answering his own question.

'The word history is the combination of two simple words – "his story". This is one of the latest findings of the leading researchers. Not just that. It has sparked such curiosity among professors the world over, that they are more interested in making history, than teaching.' Pausing for effect, Professor Dave took off his glasses and began to polish them with his handkerchief, and we, identifying a good, clean joke in the jargon, roared heartily.

'In fact, every man and woman,' a half-smile playing about his lips, he was now saying, 'is a volume of history. But those who make history have no time to write it. Had it not been so, then, all of us would have been writing and reading our own histories.'

We didn't get round to sobriety, when he sent us reeling again.

Somehow, regaining my equilibrium, I was ready with a few carefully chosen words, to thank Professor Dave for disbursing good humour, when unexpectedly, he himself lost his seriousness, proving that laughter really is infectious.

The general hysteria took more than a minute to die down.

Professor Dave had the air of a man whose knowledge of history was sound and perfect. Armed with this unshakeable conviction, he now started fiddling with history and historians.

'History has two sides; conventional and unconventional. Conventional history is fact-filled and informative, objectively useful, read in classrooms. It always involves distortion and mutilation of facts, to suit the ends of the rulers of the day.

'Unconventional history is the other side of history, the side of people, who never were the beneficiaries of these power manoeuvres, but rather, their victims. Any question?'

He waited, but the students kept quiet, while we two, were carefully neutral.

'It was not the wind or the weather that razed the temples and the artistic moments of our country. They were razed by none other than tyrannical foreign invaders. Their prime purpose was to plunder and loot the wealth of another nation and to kill those who opposed them. Their only god was wealth; their religion, a desire for it.'

With a flourish to hold the youngsters' attention, he lectured on. 'Since the dawn of history, we Indians have been unlucky and unfortunate. I can't think of a time when we were not exploited, oppressed and subjected to utter humiliation, all because India could not give a united fight. However, finally a new era came, at least now, where people were governed by the people themselves: DEMOCRACY!

'But alas! Today, after all these years of forming a democratically elected government, the whole nation is strictly ruled by the politicians who are, by and large, a bunch of fraudulent pretenders. *When democracy becomes corrupt, the best gravitates to the bottom, the worst floats to the top and vile is replaced by the more vile.'*

It seemed, with Henry George's words, he would stop fiddling with history but the indefinable character, blended with genius, went one step further.

'I want it clearly understood that history does not record itself; it is chronicled by a bought pen and perjured vision. A precedent existed in the form of the so called 'Time-capsule' that was buried in the Red Fort during the Emergency, in 1977.'

A stunning silence fell.

The well begun, colourful lecture, that went on perfectly, wouldn't have turned sour, had the professor not mixed politics with history.

We two apolitical fools got very nervous.

'What are you waiting for? Expecting some more sensational tale of unconventional history?' asked Dolly.

'God no!'

'Come on then.' And she whisked me away, using the silence that paved our way, out of this mess.

Back in the room, I said, 'Thank you, Dolly, for pulling me out of the rut.'

Dolly smiled, silently taking the credit.

'Well, it has been a fairly good day, considering everything.'

'Oh yes,' agreed Dolly, adding, 'Full of new experiences. I'd like to do it again tomorrow.'

'Thank heavens, I'm off tonight.'

'Off tonight?' She frowned in disbelief.

'Yes...To Chandigarh - that modern pilgrimage of grace and beauty.' My tone was a trifle too casual, but she didn't fail to detect the intent in it.

'What a jumpy proposition!'

'But it is a logical one.'

'Sure it is. From the decaying past to the glorious present.'

'From ruins to splendour,' I supplemented.

'And there's no denying that Chandigarh deserves our visit said Dolly, unbelievingly gay and frisky.

'Whaat!'

'Why do you yell, Sanchu? Anything serious?'

Not knowing what to say, I stared mutely at her. Just then, Naina and party, minus the boys, burst in.

'We've checked out, *didi*.'

That's rather sudden.'

Professor Dave wants us to leave now.'

'I though....'

'No *didi,* short is sweet.'

'Not always.'

'Maybe, but our *didi* is always sweet.' The youngest girl ventured.

'And so are you, my sweetie!' Dolly tweaked her cheek.

'We'll never forget our *didi.*' They trilled in unison.

'Once known never forgotten.' Dolly held out her arms to Naina.

'Sweet *didi*' said Naina, coming into Dolly's outstretched arms.

They clung, they kissed, they sobbed - the process continued to the last girl.

All women are actresses, I told myself and reached for a cigarette. Then, slowly walking over to the window, I looked out to the rose garden. The velvet-red roses, the pride of nature, caressed by the passing breeze, smiled at me.

It was when the Baroda boys' loud calls - 'Naina, Naina', well orchestrated with the throbbing foot tapping, were heard, I turned to see if they had heard what I heard. To my relief I found the melodrama had already ended and Naina's gang was about to leave.

For a second, the lot looked at me with moist eyes. Then, slowly, they started for the door. Outside the door they stopped, cast a quick look back and zoomed away, waving hands jingling with bangles.

'Sweet *didi*, goodbye!'

Those were the last words I heard from them.

Twelve

Dolly sighed a long, deep sigh and shut her eyes to hold back the tears.

A breeze, till now rustling amid the moonlit rose garden, abruptly changed its course, to visit us. It stayed one second and was gone, infecting the air with a mild, rose fragrance.

The perfumed air helped Dolly in absorbing the leftovers of the parting and also, it stimulated her to activity. First she packed the last of her belongings, then, as a gesture of friendship she packed mine.

Meanwhile, I shoved my shaving kit, toothpaste and brush into the leather pouch and zipped it. From the table where Dolly was busy packing, all of a sudden, she glanced up at me. Her eyes fastened on me and mine on hers, significantly sorting through our feelings in silence. Considerable time passed. Then -

'Well?'

The word came mild and clear. It was a vague question that didn't tell you what she expected to hear.

Lighting a cigarette, I countered with an equally vague question, 'Well, then?'

'Nothing,' she said, tossing her head in disgust.

Guessing there must be something, I remembered what I was debating with Dolly, when the Baroda girls came in, to say goodbye. Now, flicking into the ashtray, I inhaled and exhaled luxuriously before reopening the argument, for discussion.

'Dolly, would it be all right for me to ask why you want to come to Chandigarh?'

'Because I've never been there before, And...'

'And?'

'To be with you, of course!' replied Dolly saucily, but without implying too much.

'Hmmm!'

'Sanchu, you sound upset and bitter. Aren't you happy in my company?'

'It's not that, Dolly.'

'What else does it affirm?'

'Didn't you hear?' I indicated the tiny transistor on the table. 'Chandigarh is very cold this winter, the weather report said so just now.'

'Come on, Sanchu, you can think of a better excuse than that.'

'Believe me, the weather report is worrying me.'

'Okay, I believe you. But what's so unusual about it, in winter?'

'Nothing unusual. Except that I felt it's only fair to warn you.'

'Don't you worry. Nothing would happen to me as long as I am warm in your heart.' She smiled gently, but I wasn't quite sure what the mischief in her eyes meant.

She looked so gay, so eager to go on with her fun, that I could not be cross with her.

'No, no, Dolly, no. Please be serious.'

'What's there to be serious, man?' She said light-heartedly and began to smooth the wrinkles of my coat. While folding, she asked, 'Haven't we got sufficient clothes?'

'Clothes we have. But we don't have sufficient blankets.'

'I can make a suggestion if you care to heed it.'

'Suggest.'

'Well...' for a moment she paused, then walked over to the open suitcase on the table, put my coat in it and said, 'if the nights in Chandigarh are too cold, you may slip into my bed.'

Her caustic sense of humour, so calm in utterance yet so explosive in meaning, stunned me. Yet, a sharp 'what-was-that-you-said' escaped my lips.

'I know, until now, you thought me to be a *Sati Savitri*, but having said that, I have turned out to be another *Pamella Bordes*.' She gave a throaty giggle. 'So I'm no more a nice girl... Suddenly the picture of Dolly in your mind has changed.'

'Because of your immoral suggestion.'

'But what was really immoral in my suggestion? Was there any sexual desire?'

The question sounded too nasty to warrant any reply.

She waited a good ten seconds, before she alleged: 'Only a mean man maligns a friendly gesture.'

This outrageous allegation shook me, from head to foot.

'Dolly!' So loud I roared in a raging anger that my voice got choked. Even then, the words came marching into my mind, like deadly soldiers. *Was there ever a woman who slept with a man under one blanket keeping off sex? Was there ever a man who escaped that eternal fire?* They shaped in my mouth, ready for speaking. But my tongue refused to articulate a single word; stiffened, it lay prostrate, flexibility totally lost, as if the sudden growth of a bone had made it inoperative.

After moments of gloomy silence, unrepentant Dolly muttered:

'Most men see women as sex objects.'

'But there's no avoiding the obvious, in a delicate situation like that.'

'Why can't a man and a woman come closer in honesty and confidence? Why does it have to be sex only?' She asked with veiled accusation in her voice.

For a moment I wondered: *Was she psychologically imbalanced in the matter of sex, or thoroughly Americanised? Or was she providing me ample rope to hang myself?*

In the midst of this uncomfortable situation we had to fall silent or risk spoiling our relationship, whether it was love, respect, earthly intimacy, whatever it was, that had grown, slowly and steadily, since the first moment our eyes met.

A significant pause later, Dolly, her eyes batting and a half smile playing about her lips, said, 'For nothing you became serious - it depends on who I am with,' and she resumed packing.

The silence closed in again.

In direct proportion to the pace of her thinking, she herself broke the silence.

'Why do you make a difference between male and female? *Prana* is common to both the sexes; only external features differ. It all depends on the chemistry; that is the hormones. According to our Hindu mythology, God is a combination of both.'

'However much you may entice me, I won't give in.'

'I'm not enticing, just reasoning.' A thin smile spread on her lips. 'Why do you misinterpret a comradely gesture?'

'Because I don't want to repent later.'

'Neither do I. But a little act of sharing and caring certainly wouldn't make us unholy,' she said magnanimously.

'If bedding under one blanket is a little act of sharing and caring, God save me.'

'Nature created men and women not to live apart but for sharing and caring.'

'Not until the man and woman are recognised as husband and wife.'

'Whom do you distrust? The man or the woman?' She gave me a notoriously curious smile.

'I am afraid I can't answer that.'

'Don't hedge, Sanchu,' she said warningly.

'Honestly, Dolly, I am not hedging. I don't know the answer. That's all.'

While we were locked in a serious argument there was a cautious rapping on the door. For a second we stared at each other. Again, there was a mild rap.

'Answer,' I told Dolly.

'Who's that?' she called.

'Me, Jaggu.'

'It's open. Come in.'

Soundlessly, the Happy Home room boy came in. He stood for a moment, then walked to where our luggage lay. He picked up the travelbags and went out of the door, as silently as he came in.

Dolly snapped the last suitcase shut and spoke to herself, 'What's the use?' Her tone suggested a kind of despair. Walking slowly and heavily to the window, she peered out, hoping to receive a reply from the roses, bathing in the moonlight.

A rosy quest!

For some moments I kept looking at her. Suddenly I felt like having a cigarette. I dug the 'Charms' packet out from my pocket, gave it some tapping and shaking, but it produced none. Not even a speck of tobacco dust. My desire for a cigarette turned to disgust

- I crumpled the empty packet into a ball and threw it out into the garden.

Standing motionless, with her eyes glued on the blooming roses, Dolly was drifting in the sea of her thoughts. As the flying paper ball hit the rosebud, she turned round. Her eyes, misted with tears, censured me. They told so much; they held so much pain. In them, by now, two tears, large and warm, had gradually welled up. They rolled down her cheeks. Just the two.

A twinge of unaccustomed pity moved me. Taking a slow step forward, I advanced towards her. She lowered her gaze to the floor to hide the tears. Reaching near enough to touch her, I wanted to ask, what is it this time, that brought tears in your eyes? Instead, I reined myself, still debating on how to ask.

Considerably later, regaining control of herself, Dolly looked up, a faint smile crossed her saddened face.

Boosted by her faint smile, I tried to cheer her up, with a brighter one, but it failed to evoke the intended response.

Dolly sighed. Then she mumbled to herself, 'No man can possibly measure the depth of a woman's grief.'

'It's a pity of course, but being so beautiful you shouldn't bother yourself about it.'

'Whaaat?' She stared hard at me.

'Easy,' I told her not to fuss. 'I meant you're beautiful, that's all.'

'Have you only just discovered it?'

'Need a born beauty be discovered by a raw, like me?'

'May be not. But still...'

'A poet only can answer that. In my eyes you're more beautiful than...than...'

'Than?'

'Those roses swaying on their slender stems.'

She was smiling now, through the tears. Then, blushing suddenly, she said, 'Lies, lies, all lies,' and cuddled her face into my chest.

I hugged her tightly. 'Then I don't know how to convince you.'

'You don't have to. I'm so happy,' Dolly said, melting. 'It's nice to know you like the way I look.'

Carelessly running my right forefinger on her slender shoulder, I placated Dolly, 'God really took time when He created you!' And the odd thing was, all of a sudden, I started feeling romantic. In the past, I had defined such spells defined as the aura of unrequited love.

'Oh, Sanchu! I'm so glad,' drugged by my praise, she repeated, 'I'm so glad.' In the exuberance of the moment, her eyes lit up. Then, flinging her arms around me, she got eloquent: 'We haven't known each other long, but my mind tells me that you won't be going to Chandigarh without me.'

'That's a fine, female intuition indeed.'

'Come, come Sanchu, let's not quibble about intuition. You must know, I didn't join this excursion to see you from here. I go where you go - that's final. Another thing. Here onwards all the bills shall be footed by me. Okay?'

'Okay. Okay. You win.'

After that, all disputes and disagreements dissolved in affection.

Thirteen

The train whistle's warning blasts shrieked through the morning calm, before entering Chandigarh Railway Station, camouflaged in fog.

Dolly, smartly donned in blue jeans and red sweater, fresh and radiant after a wash and brush of her face and hair, pulled a tiny silver compact, a lipstick and a phial of Venus V perfume from her bag. First she retouched her lipstick carefully, then dabbed perfume behind her ears, wrists and throat, delicately. While she was admiring herself in the compact mirror, the tantalising scent of the perfume began tickling my nostrils.

It was more than a minute now, jerkily slowing down, the train had stopped. And yet, there was no sign of any porter, which seemed rather unusual, because the porters are expected to reach the passengers long before the train halts - a normal practice everywhere that seldom varies.

Just when, giving up all hopes, I was going to tug the suitcase from the rack, a porter arrived. Without a word, he picked up our luggage and started for the door.

Much relieved, less pleased, we allowed ourselves to be led by him. But, the moment we got off, we were blinded by the thick fog that had completely blotted out the platform. *So, it was Mr Fog, the villian, who had delayed the porter*, I mused.

Nothing could be seen beyond a finger's breath. Even then, slowly and cautiously, I followed the porter, with Dolly gripping me tightly by the arm. The lights on the platform had turned the fog into a white, wreathing cloud. We walked past them, stumbling.

After trudging along for nearly five minutes, we came to a bus stand. There was already a scramble among the tiny tots for the window seats.

Dolly, forgetting her age, joined the scramble and eventually we were unable to get seats together. All were seated except a little girl, who almost missed the bus. She came crying to Dolly and insisted that she, being older, should make room for her.

Her cry touched Dolly's usual kind nature. Quickly getting aside, she let her share her seat with a sisterly smile.

'Thank you,' said the little one in a watery voice.

'Oh, don't mention it, cutie!' said Dolly, stooping to kiss her.

Brushing her tear-filled eyes, the girl smiled at her and two missing teeth in her upper jaw made her smile all the more endearing.

Children are children. It is the same everywhere. They have no prejudices. They are direct in their relations with people. Often I'm attracted by their spontaneity. Rapt in thought, I barely realised that the bus had roared out of the stand, onto the empty road.

In the blinding, foggy morning, after a mile's smooth run, the driver braked sharply, narrowly averting a head-on collision with a speeding lorry. At that unwarned moment, drivers often lost control and he did. The bus, dashing into a roadside tree, stopped. Luckily no one was hurt, only the radiator was badly dented.

Even before the deadly shock could be absorbed, to everyone's relief a *chaiwalla* materialised from the darkness, with a huge kettle of steaming, hot tea and soon we found ourselves sipping and gossiping.

Within minutes a repair van arrived. Two men in overalls, a mechanic and his helper, leapt out and set to work speedily. First they replaced the damaged radiator, then they checked the engine.

After falsely reporting the breakdown as a minor accident, they called up the company's repair shop from a nearby public telephone. All this time the bus driver stood motionless, with a shade of guilt on his face. He was warned by the mechanic, 'Drive safely,' while his helper mocked him with 'We wouldn't come next time,' and they got into the waiting van and gunned away.

The driver, before climbing into his cabin, let loose a flood of vicious invective at the fast disappearing van, profusely polluting the fresh, morning air. Then he gave the door an ear-splitting slam and dropped himself into the driver's seat. He was filled with as much shame as fury. Pulling half a *badshahi bidi* from behind his ear, he lit it, drew at it deeply, through a cupped fist and blew out a cloud of blue smoke. Thus easing his tension, he shook his head, gripping the steering wheel tight.

The driver, cool now, turned the ignition key. With engine running, twice he honked, indicating the end of the halt. Visibility was still poor. After a couple of kilometres of slow and cautious driving, as the feeling of confidence began to return, he increased speed.

By now, the swirling fog had started thinning. Shapes of trees emerged like ghosts huddling in the cold and a weak sun was trying to push through the low, hanging clouds. When the fifteen kilometres run ended at Corbu's town, that irrefutable evidence of a grand piece of progress, all breathed in happiness.

There is something in the very air of Chandigarh that makes old people young and young people younger. The famous architect, the late Le Corbusier, took full advantage of the landscape, to beautify the town. A green belt, stretching from one end of the town to the other, was remarkable.

With Dolly on the pillion, I went round the 'Paradise of Northern India' on a hired scooter, that purred like a kitten and fled like a wild stallion. Wide concrete roads, excellent and meticulously laid and ribbon straight, had no caution boards nor a board showing curves anywhere. Only a stern sign bearing this warning: STRAIGHT ROAD. DRIVERS DON'T SLEEP – was prominently displayed, at rings of the main roads and intersections.

Chandigarh, the garden city of Punjab, is a tribute to the talent of an architect who infused ideals of style and beauty, in every stick and stone. Le Corbusier, the genius behind this architectural splendour, believed in 'Sun, Space and Verdure' which fashion our body and spirit and without which man is isolated from his natural environment. For healthy living, Le Corbusier re-established nature, blending town and country, until senseless stones and masonry melted into gardens and parks, and man and Nature were harmonised as of yore.

To our bad luck, in the heart of this modern town, our two-wheeler came to a dead stop, for want of gas.

First she exchanged a glance with me, then swore, before setting her feet on the ground.

'Get the tank refuelled. Don't take too long. I'll be waiting right here,' she commanded in the tones of a drill sergeant.

'At your service, Madam.' Bowing to her stern order, I left for a filling station.

Coming back directly to the same spot after refuelling, I found Dolly not quite her usual self; rather in a state of tense expectation and waiting to erupt, which only lent evidence to her seriousness. But her frequently changing mood also provided the grounds for not taking her seriousness seriously.

Leaving the scooter under the shade of a roadside tree, I strode across the lawn. When she was only ten steps away, deliberately I coughed to be heard for attention. But it went unheard. Acting on a naughty idea that had suddenly struck me, I moved closer, tiptoeing. Halting one step behind, I cupped her eyes.

Quick as lightning, Dolly's hands flashed up, grabbed my wrist, flicked me over her shoulder – all in one fluid motion.

Sprawled on the ground, while still reeling from the shock, horror and humiliation, sprinting, she came over to me, heartless and violent, with her right foot raised, but I was too fast, to roll over.

'What are you up to, Dolly? Gone mad?'

The question put her into a dilemma. An etched frown burrowed into her forehead. She put down the right foot that was about to stomp me. Then, shaking her head in disbelief, she took a closer look at my face gently, to shriek 'He, not you!' finding it was me.

'He – who?' A suspicion was born and died within me in the same moment.

Emotionally unstable, she was now wailing at the top of her lungs. 'O Ma, what have I done? What have I done?'

Before I accepted the reality of this rudest of shocks, I was on my feet again. Although heart-broken I escaped unhurt, except for a bruise on my neck.

Slowly, piecing together my broken heart, bit by bit, as I focussed my eyes in her direction, the shock, the confusion, the emptiness and the sadness... unitedly fed the anger inside me.

'What style! What accuracy! What fluidity!' The dread words came softly at least; then went about transmitting wrath. 'This is how a karate expert handles an enemy, not a friend. Total strangers, when we started this journey. Turned into devoted friends, hour by hour. Then suddenly this deadly assualt. How could you do this to me? Inconceivable!

'But strange are the ways of women. It's heart-breaking coming from someone, from whom I expect understanding and friendship. Nevertheless, this unique experience will go into my lasting memories. I can't imagine anyone in his or her right mind, can behave this brutally. May be, to give a new meaning to the word 'friendship'.

'There we were, all nice and cosy. Now looking at what happened I'm forced to think – it's all over. And finally, we're at a point to say…'

'No!' she strongly protested. 'Without giving me a chance to defend myself, I won't let you dismiss me so summarily.'

'Yes, I can and I will. There's no feeling, no sensation left, Dolly. Nothing. Oh, what a friend you turned out to be!'

Her heart soaked with sorrow and face paled with shame, Dolly, hoping for a reprieve, pleaded, 'I feel inexplicable sorry for what happened.'

'Whatsoever or however! No compromise.'

'I admit that under tense, emotional, untenable circumstances friendship can turn into hatred. But by denying me a fair hearing, you'll never know why did I do it.'

Now, being an open-minded man, I didn't want to dismiss her without listening to her tale.

'Ok, I'll grant you that.' Reluctantly I relented, still dazed by what she had done.

Gaining the concession, her eyes thanked me. Then, taking a deep breath, she began to relate what had happened during my short absence.

'After you left for refuelling, I was feeling terribly alone. But, very soon I became lost in my immediate surrounding…'

'Hello beautiful, all alone?' From behind, a distant male voice startled me.

Even though I sensed danger, I didn't care to turn around to see who he was, or how he looked. The sly talk and slow approach spoke all about the man's intention. For tricking him into thinking that I was one for the game, I played:

'Yeah, all alone.'

'Maybe you'd like my company?'

'You'll regret' was my unspoken reply.

A deserted place… a good-looking young girl… content with his lucky find, he was coming faster now like a bear, for honey. The two and a half years of karate lessons may now prove worthwhile, I thought and waited, with bated breath.

'Let's go to some hotel…I'll treat you to a coffee.'

He had, by now, come within striking distance. Judging this as the right moment for action, I threw an explosive kick in his groin. With a loud 'Oomp' he fell to his knees, as the air gushed from his gaping mouth. For a brief moment it looked as if he was not going to get up. Surprisingly, however, soon he scrambled to his feet to run for dear life.

'Well, that's that,' she ended the shocking incident with great coolness. 'You can't just believe that, can you?'

'Believing apart, it makes no sense.'

'Since when 'making sense' had any serious reference to what happens in reality?'

'But there must be a connection between what you did to me and what happened to you.'

'There's,' she said gravely. 'Anticipation that the attacker would return, the recurrence of the incident was dreaded. At that precise moment, your uncharacteristic, lovely way of blocking my eyes deceived me and I mistook you, for him.' Pausing for a moment, she asked politely, 'Now, do I make myself clear?'

'Oh yes, abundantly clear.'

'I'm terribly sorry.'

'That's one way of dealing with a rogue. You should be proud, not apologetic. If I were you, I would have done the same thing.'

'But – but, Sanchu, a happening of that kind…' She buried her head in her hands. The tears of overwhelming grief that had already filled her eyes now started creeping down her cheeks.

'Don't cry.' I whisked my handkerchief out and wiped her tears. 'In the circumstances what choice did you have?'

'Sanchu, you don't have any idea, deep down inside, how I'm feeling.'

'No use thinking about it now. As far as I'm concerned it never happened.'

'O-h-h, Sanchu! You're really great. I never knew such a thorough gentleman existed in these days of ours.'

Mind you, some gentlemen are experts in the art of changing women's opinions.'

'Oh, really?'

'After all, a gentleman is also a human.'

'That means you also can.'

'Everything has its moments, you know!'

'You smooth-talking rascal! I'll kill you.'

'But luckily I'm already dead.'

Almost instantly, the sagging threat between us tightened and we laughed, a loud joyful laugh, moving into each other's arms.

A passing old man, having mistaken us for a honeymooning couple, stopped to say, 'Congratulations!' and moved on, smiling at some memory of his own.

To our bad luck, the rare spell of fine, intimate moments that we were then sharing, was murdered by the incessant ringing of bicycle bells.

Frightfully, tearing away from me, she caught sight of three under-fifteen bikers, ringing bells cheekily, grinning from ear to ear.

'You spoilt brats!' Dolly shouted, shaking her fists at them

The inexperienced eve-teasers were badly shaken, unaccustomed as they were, to being called brats. Waving bye-bye, they cycled away to safety. But looking at the way they were fleeing from Dolly's wrath, I couldn't stop laughing.

'What sort of man are you? Everything is spoilt and you're laughing.'

'It's unfair to be angry. They are, after all, kids.'

'Kids, huh! Today's twelve-year-olds are more grown-up than you can imagine.'

'May be a few – not many.'

'Many- though not all.'

Dolly was stupidly stubborn.

'You argue too, damn, much, like today's so-called educated woman. You know I'm right.' With that, I turned and stalked off.

I had barely gone twenty paces, Dolly came running and taking my hand said, 'You 're dead right, Mr Right.' Then nestling against me, she cooed, 'I don't know why I'm always wrong.'

This minute she was the naughtiest little thing; next minute she was perfectly innocent. And that, I think, is exactly why I liked her.

'But Miss Wrong, what makes you hold my hand like this?'

'For a good feeling and better intimacy...' her eyes were guiltless, a smile at the corners, her grip tightened.

Like lovers we walked on, arm in arm, immersed in our own thoughts, till we reached the Parliament, a square assembly building; an eight-hundred foot long Secretariat, eight storeys high; a small square Governor's place and several, related elements of landscaping on different levels; finally, the 'Monument of the Open Hand'. After going over all these buildings, we slowly turned towards the Hall of Justice.

The irregular concrete vaults which, however, fit into the Modular scale (a huge parasol of concrete shades the building properly) a concrete, roof umbrella, sheltering a four-storeyed, entrance lobby, lined with concrete ramps and topped by arches... A brilliant work of imagination, the Hall of Justice.

Bothered by her habitual curiosity, Dolly tugged at my sleeve. 'Sanchu, when was the Hall of Justice completed?'

'Around nineteen fifty, if my memory serves me right.'

'How deceptive! To me it appears to be very old.'

'Yes, that's the matter of art. Here Corbu has achieved the timelessness that will make his architecture a permanent treasure of man's history. The concrete exterior, in all unfinished roughness, has emerged, looking as wonderfully coarse as a rock formation, moulded by thousands of years of wind and rain. This piece of 'March Forward' is a gift to India, through the master-hand of Corbu, understandable in terms of both the past and the present and prophetic of the future.'

'Who was Corbu?'

'The great French architect whose services were hired by the Punjab Government vis-à-vis the Government of India.'

'But why had the Government chosen a Frenchman, instead of giving this rare opportunity to a deserving Indian?' A rhetorical question if ever there was one.

With no more argument I led the way to the High Court.

The High Court, distinguished from its surroundings by a clock tower, sat in the middle of vast, manicured lawns, that were dotted with symmetrical, evenly spaced flower beds. As we entered the great courtrooms, Dolly, enthralled by the exquisite interior, could hardly resist her excitement.

'Gee, these are fantastic!'

I was delighted to see her happy, but it quickly changed to scorn, as she threw her arms around my neck.

'What the hell are you doing?'

'Trying to make our memorable tour a little more delicious,' and she was about to kiss me.

In time, with a restrained hand on her mouth, I checked her.

Don't waste such a precious commodity on a worthless *fakir*. Save it for your young millionaire.'

Her enthusiasm was dampened.

'You're an extremely shy man, Sanchu.' Curving her mouth in a mirthless smile, she remarked. 'Don't worry. I only expressed my feelings about Corbu, not that I intend to do it, to you. Do you think I am so insensible?'

'I'm glad that you have some sense.'

'Sense is not anybody's property that I shouldn't have some. Every one of us shares this gift from God.'

Not to become too involved in Dolly's verbal fencing, I changed the subject.

'Look there.' I pointed diagonally across the flying ramps connecting the various levels of the building. 'No ascending or descending of stairs... just an easy walk to reach any floor. Balconies, arches and columns, wherever you look. They offer new, unexpected, delightful, spatial experiences.'

'Great was your Corbu and this piece of his art shows that he was a passionately, emotional man.'

'You've said it,' with reverence for Corbu, I spoke out aloud. 'There is no art without emotion, no emotion without passion.

Stones are dead things sleeping in the quarries. He brought life into them, to live on through those dead stones.'

'Strange!' she exclaimed in surprise. 'Sanchu, you speak at times, like an architect.'

'That's nothing strange, my dear. Writer and architect, both deal in creative ideas, though their areas are different. The two are synonymous.'

'In other words, both are creative geniuses.'

'Don't delude yourself into thinking that I'm a genius.'

'No. It is a fact, not a delusion.'

'But of course I understand that your Corbu was a great architect who enjoyed worldwide recognition. Whereas my Corbu is a poor writer, still awaiting some recognition.'

'Your Corbu!'

'Yes. Why? Can't I have a Corbu?'

'So you're making fun of me.'

'No. I swear.' The wonder girl suddenly lifted my hand to her lips. 'You're my Corbu. I love you.'

'Emotions! Sentiments! Love! Please don't scatter them, as you like,' I cautioned her.

That was like cautioning the Niagara to fall more slowly.

'My Corbu! My Corbu! My Corbu!' She clung to me madly and held me tight, with fierce possessiveness. 'Believe it or not, Sanchu, right now, my feminine instincts say differently. A little dancing, some drinking; I'm ready for anything you can dream up and more.'

Revolting at her emotional outburst, I pushed her away with both hands. 'To hell with your female instincts. I hate scenes.'

She hadn't fully sobered herself yet and laughed derisively. 'Acting *Vivekanada!*'

'Stop exporting love epidemic!'

'I despise those who are completely refined,' a slighted Dolly retorted.

'I don't mind if you women despise me for that.'

'You're a fool.'

'I think you are the one who's behaving foolishly.'

'Sanchu, when will you learn to colour life a bit, instead of filling it with nothing but ideals?'

'Don't bother, Miss Bombay. I am all right as I am.'

'I will also see, Mr Vivekanand, how long it's going to be like this,' Dolly's eyes challenged me and she left it at that.

Thus we moved into the Assembly Hall, a wonderful play of concrete cubes against free-form elements, also of concrete.

It is well said that if you are not charmed at the first sight of the new capital of the Punjab, then you haven't eyes to see.

Sampling almost all the sensual, architectural splendours that Chandigarh had to offer, hungry and weary, we rushed to the shop, to return the scooter.

'Here, let me help you,' said a mechanic, taking the tiny transport aside, for checking. In the meantime, I reached the counter to pay the hire charges.

Looking at the huge tip that I had added, the owner-cum cashier said, 'If it's all right with you, I'll take it.'

'Thanks.'

And we laughed together, shaking hands. He was obviously amazed at my ingenuity.

On the way out as Dolly held my hand tightly, I said, 'You must be very hungry.'

'Now that you mention it, I'm absolutely famished.'

Not surprisingly, just as in babies, hunger was reflected on her face.

Fourteen

It was then a quarter past two

Nearest to the shop, the lovely restaurant, 'Park View', beckoned us. A smartly uniformed man guarding the entrance, which was coolly shaded beneath an awning, gave Dolly a royal salute, as she entered.

Some women walk into restaurants, while others make entrances. Dolly emphatically belonged to the latter group and her entrance invariably was spectacular. From the way the waiters deferred to her, all male heads turned to this new, valued client.

The headwaiter led us to a table for two, in a cosy corner, in the 'moonlight' room, a special room where light and shade blended rhythmically with the soft music playing from hidden speakers.

'Order what you like,' I told Dolly, without looking at the menu.

'Oh, you're so nice.'

Quickly running her eyes down the menu she sent away the headwaiter, ordering two regular vegetarian *thaalis*.

'Now what has suddenly gone wrong?' I enquired anxiously.

'Nothing. Studying the prices on the menu, I declined to make use of your generous offer.'

'Who asked you to worry your head about the prices?'

'Now, Sanchu, you're acting like a young millionaire.'

'Contamination.' I tossed off the unkind remark with one word.

'Contamination?' Dolly's brow puckered in puzzlement.

'Means tainted by association with a rich, pampered girl.' The last three words, though spoken in a whisper, were easily deciphered caught by her, from my lip movement.

'You!' She brandished a clenched fist, pouting in mock anger.

That's when the head waiter reappeared followed by a young waiter wheeling a trolley. They hurried away, serving our order dexterately.

As we were hungry beyond expression, we hogged it all in rapid haste, not even once looking at each other, Surprisingly, our table manners, too, had deserted us.

Lunch over, while we were waiting to be served coffee, a hefty *Haryanvi*, a plate heaped high with food before him, was slyly looking at Dolly. My look told him to take his eyes off her. In reply his eyes mocked me. I read his mind: *Buddy this town is our town, we run it. What we say goes. And you two, are strangers. If you try to be oversmart, I will show you your place. And don't bother about police protection. The police do what we say. Now use your head.*

There wasn't anything I could do, other than turn my head. Keeping the thought to myself I lit a cigarette, but was overwhelmingly conscious of his hard eyes watching me. Quickly and nervously, puffing at my cigarette and then blowing out bluish clouds of smoke, I tried vainly to create a smokescreen between us.

The coffee arrived.

Taking a sip as I looked up, I observed anger flaring in Dolly's eyes. Amused I asked, 'What happened?'

Leaning forward, she spoke in hushed tone. 'That man at the table directly opposite. Every time I look up, I find his eyes on me.'

'I, too, have noticed – just ignore him.'

'But that wouldn't stop him.'

'Don't be so upset and miserable. That would embolden him further.'

'Ha!' Eyeing him defiantly, Dolly sipped her coffee and tried to appear calm.

I finished my coffee and casually turned to the man. To my amazement I found that his eyes were still riveted on her and his gaze was now so bold and so provocative that I had the odd feeling he knew exactly what Dolly looked like, stark-naked.

'He's positively indecent.'

'Indecent is hardly the word.' Dolly's face was aflame with anger. 'Raper – that's the only word for it.'

At this moment the man was once again in Dolly's direct line of vision. A devilish smile was playing around his mouth and his eyes held an undisguised challenge.

Dolly's fist clenched, her blood boiling. 'I feel like giving him one in the eye.'

'Control yourself,' I urged. 'He isn't the only one ogler. All eyes are fastened on you; can't you see?'

Dolly's eyes roved the elegant lunch room.

'Yes, I do see. In a way they're right.'

'Right?'

'Don't you see they're eating the same food under the same roof?'

'Emmm…I can see that! It's quite in character.'

'In the circumstances we should leave. Immediately!' She scraped back her chair and stood up. Her face was like a thundercloud.

'Hey, wait a minute.'

'No!' She said firmly and started crossing the carpeted lunch room. Most puzzling to my eyes, her buttock was moving lightly with accentuated grace, but by no means in deliberate display. All eyes had now turned in her direction. As uncaring as ever, she glided out of the restaurant in a silent stride; then with uneasy haste, she began to walk along the footpath.

I frowned for some seconds and wondered for the hundredth time, if she was a crackpot. Then, I called the waiter and paid the bill.

After I came out of the restaurant I had to jog to catch up with her. Breathless beside her, I asked:

'Where do you think you're running like that?'

'To hell. Follow me if you must.' She made a scornful face.

'But why the hell do you want to go to hell?'

'That's entirely my own business,' her terse reply annoyed me.

'Then – go.' I gave her a slight push.

Dolly, livid with rage, could not speak a word, for half a minute. Then, she blazed:

'Sanchu!'

'Dolly!' I snapped. 'Keep your temper under control. I, too, have a right to get angry.'

'Nooooooo!' She screamed, bursting into tears. 'You've no right to get angry.'

Puzzled, I looked searchingly into her eyes. No spark. No glow. No charm either. Just dull and dim, two tired eyes bulging with the strain of travel.

'What's the matter, Dolly? Not feeling well?'

'What do you care, Mr Globe-trotter?'

'I'm sorry. You must be worn out. Why don't you rest a little?'

'Yes.' Dolly, in her moment of rage and grief, smothered a yawn. 'That's what I'm going to do.'

The Central Park was directly across the street. A number of limousines were parked at the curb.

At a slow and halting pace we entered the park – one of the pleasant spots of Chandigarh, where everything was very still, blended with a subtle aura of sublimity.

Under a shady, mango tree we sat on the lush carpet of green. Then, nestling against me, Dolly said in a sleepy voice:

'Sanchu, you realise that I haven't tried to find out anything about you.'

'That's because you don't doubt about my being a nameless nobody.'

'No-oo –you're kidding. Anyway, can I regard you as a friend?'

'Yes. Of course we're friends; so far we haven't had much time to show it.'

'Good. That gives me confidence. Suppose I now take an hour's nap on your lap – for friendship's sake?'

I smiled, by way of consent.

'How lucky I'm to have met you.' Blinding me with her thousand-watt grin, she slipped an arm around me. Then, letting her other arm go around the shoulder, she held me close. But, before I realised what was happening, it happened. Like a vice her lips were already clamped on mine, while her body passionately entwined mine.

After a few, fiery moments I struggled free. 'You lovesick oaf!'

The steely words delivered in an anguished undertone, made no dent on her.

'A chance like this doesn't come along very often.' She grinned a wicked grin.

'You little fraud!' I raised a clenched fist and was about to swing at her when she, closing her eyelids, swayed into my lap.

'Call me anything. I did what I like doing.'

'But your young millionaire won't like it.'

'He won't know, unless you tell him.'

'I won't, if you promise to behave like a good girl, hereafter.'

She promised.

Some time passed before either of us spoke again.

'Sanchu,' it was a mere whisper, 'Don't you know anything about women?'

'The less I know, the better.'

'Perhaps, that is why, you're so trusting where women are concerned.'

Drawing the safety curtain, she lapsed into an exhausted slumber.

It was way past high noon, at its most somnolent.

Fifteen

Waking refreshed, after an hour's nap, Dolly's arms impulsively went up around my neck and she was hanging on me as hangs a row of pearls upon its strings.

Her romance-in-the-open sparked off a galore of wolf whistles.

Startled, Dolly asked, 'Who whistled?'

As if in reply to her question, an avalanche of paper arrows fell upon her, from all directions, accompanied by loud boos.

She sat up in a shot, looked around and said, 'Sanchu, look at those jealous eyes.'

'I have been seeing them all the while, now you see.'

She studied those inspecting eyes. She did not object. Rather, she endured them.

They were college students, come here to spend their free period.

As time passed, my face must have shown bitterness and discontent.

'What bites you my friend? Are you dying for single love?' She teased me and I bounced it back with spin:

'My dear, games always start with 'Love-all'…and if it's your beginning, ask them to come to you.'

'Goodness Gracious!' Dolly jumped to her feet, brushing the grass and dirt off her clothes, she asked, 'Are they all modern *Heer Ranjhas?'*

'Not at all, Miss Romantic,' one from the crowd slyly replied, 'but a good many of us, may be.'

A wave of laughter swept the ground, then another and another.

I looked at them contemptuously. In return, the boys cast on me one of their frozen, don't-care-a-damn looks, whereas the girls went giddy, with anticipation.

The situation was hotting up fast, and was about to take an ugly turn. It was a real tight spot, beyond escape. But yet, bright ideas on escape, old and new, flooded my mind and deciding one I told those collegians:

'I've a thrilling announcement to make,' to which an unexpected quiet descended upon them. They were still quiet when I made the sensational announcement. 'The Disco Queen is now going round the town. Ladies and gentlemen wanting autographs can join in her round-the-town-parade, ending in front of the Town Hall.'

The students burst into loud cheers. In contrast, Dolly looked at me, with hostility.

'This is nothing but deliberate degradation.'

'Don't overreact,' I counselled prudence. 'Just give them your autograph.'

'You stupid fool! When the situation demands skilful handling, you expect me to hand out autographs?'

Feeling both ashamed and foolish, I was grimly silent. Words, that were the tools of my trade would not come to defend me.

Upon seeing the crowd slowly surging forward, Dolly's fear tripped her anger.

'What a mess we're in! You got me into this. Now you sort things out.'

Like the shattering of glass, Dolly's anger and scorn began to splinter about me, while my jammed mind was unable to determine the right action in the crisis.

The solution presented itself to me suddenly, when I remembered what I had once been told by Inder: *The Northerners, coarse by nature, could be restrained only by a showdown.* Ready in an instant, with uprolled sleeves, as I was about to make a dash, Dolly held me back with a firm grip on my wrist.

'Have you gone off your head? I didn't think you're that insane, Sanchu.'

'Let me go.'

'I surely don't need to remind you, how dangerous it is.'

'Are you trying to scare me?'

'Don't be an idiot. I'm appealing to your good sense, that's all.'

'No matter what happens to me, I must teach them a lesson.' My hands balled into fists and I stood obstinately erect. My prestige was at stake.

'What's on your mind, Sanchu?' This time, with a deadly calm, she asked, 'Want to go to hospital?'

Struck by the seriousness of her tone, as I looked around, the don't-care-lot stared at me, in defiance. My conscience beeped, causing muscle spasm on my face. Dolly, having noticed it, whispered;

'Relax; I'll tackle them.' Then, releasing my hand, she took a step forward and turned her palms to the student, in appeal. The sudden twist that she gave to the scene was more by instinct, than by reasoning.

Magically, the advancing, irate students halted, at an honourable distance.

The crush and rumble of falling vanity transformed the carefree boaster, to a mere onlooker.

And now, wearing her principal weapon, the 32-carat smile, she addressed the crowd:

'Instead of a boy finding himself on a bench with a beautiful girl, a girl is meeting many handsome boys, in a park. No wonder, the world is fast changing.'

Elated by Dolly's romantic approach, one quoted:

'Change is a function of time.'

'And time is on our side,' another dequoted.

The famous line, now distortingly presented, greatly vexed me. But the distortion was quite lost, on Dolly. She reproved the mob with calm dignity.

'No nonsense, please.'

That did it.

The students' behaviour was electrically regulated.

For a while all was quiet on the student front: and I, taking advantage of the lull, advocated:

'Be good citizens.'

But my advocacy gave a new outlet for tumult.

'Of course we are!' The isolated protest was supported by a boastful chorus.

'Good! Splendid!' Cheered Dolly to avert fresh trouble. 'That's what the world expects its youth to be.'

'What about your round-the-town-parade, Miss Disco Queen?' Someone wanted to know.

Dolly's brow knotted, eyes narrowed into slits. Perhaps she was weighing out the chances of escaping the obscurity, that I had shoved her into.

It just wouldn't be right if, in her most embarrassing moment, you remained silent, my guilty conscience admonished.

To right the wrong, quickly reacting, as I urged the students, 'My good friends, if only for a moment listen to me…' A loose abuse 'Bastard! Acting important', was thrown on me. Undeterred, I went on, 'Before I give you the benefit of the slip of my lips, I'd like to explain things, a but…'

'We don't want any explanation,' a rough voice cut me short.

'And no tricking,' someone added and many reiterated.

'I think this Johnny is trying to cancel the parade,' a girl fuelled it further.

'Nothing doing!' Threatening with his fist up, a giant Sikh warned, 'Don't you dare cancel the parade,' and the collegians roared their approval.

Dolly, who was standing at my side quietly till then, assessing the situation, now confronted the hostile students with a proud smile.

'On the contrary, this is the time to put principle aside and do what my friend had announced earlier.'

'Then why this waste of time?' The whole battalion of students looking distinctly impatient, demanded.

I was at my wits' end to size up the situation and began counting my heartbeats, when an extraordinary thing happened.

'Come and follow me!' A militant Dolly, very much new in shape and look, gave a battle cry, with all the power of her lungs before she was on the march.

Sixteen

The stunned students clicked their heels and solemnly raised their arms, in Hitlerian style.

Pride flung back the head of this modern Joan of Arc, as she took the Nazi salute and steered the student brigade out into the street. Ramrod straight, head held high, she was walking a bit ahead of all, carrying an imaginary banner. She had a peculiar grace of motion that was swift, tense and oddly enough, challengingly feminine.

How quickly she had reacted: there was no predicting what she might do, next. I marvelled at her manipulative skill that shook the students, pushing them beyond anything they had imagined. Probably, fear and anger gave way to a scheme, such as this.

Just like the lame boy who was left behind, in the procession led by the Pied Piper of Hamelin, I was the only one abandoned in the park. Moments later, my legs involuntarily began to move, as if someone had whipped them, to give them momentum. I still had a lot of ground to cover and was wondering what measure to adopt, when the signal light at the intersection of the street, changed to red bringing the merry procession to a halt.

By the time I joined the modern Joan of Arc, the traffic light turned green. Almost immediately, 'Ooh-la-la!' the three magic syllables burst from the processioninsts' lips like savage barks and the merry procession started to move again.

Now the roadside crowds roared in jubilation, as Dolly whirled round, blowing kisses to them.

By now she had mesmerised one and all. Taking with her the student brigade, she danced and dazzled her way to the Main Square. To the delight of the long-waiting, massive crowd, she introduced herself; 'Hello everybody! I'm Dolly, new in your town.'

The tens and thousands of Chandigarhians who had cordoned the area from all sides, now greeted her with a full throated 'Ooh-la-la!

'It is exciting to be here with you. I have never before seen such a huge crowd as this. I'll never forget…'

'Dolly, you're welcome.' The crowd roared in adulation.

Those in the terraces threw flowers at her. From the mob, down the street, many adorned her, with garlands. Simultaneously, rose a deafening shout of great joy: 'Dolly, we adore you!'

'Friends, I've no past nor am I crazy about the future. I delight in the present.' Continuing in the same vein, she added, 'My world is filled with love and laughter; fun is the thing I'm after.'

'Cye Balle! Balle' balle!!!' Once again the crowd, wild with excitement, lustily cheered her.

This time, the cheering was much longer and louder than the previous one.

'Sing along! Today is your day. Your opportunity.'

Dolly's 'go-gay' call though, raised the jolly townsmen's spirit high, the anticipated reaction did not come off. It was then the dancing beauty gave a flash-dance from her audience winning arsenal, leaping and spinning, keeping balance supremely well. Without any hint of stopping, she just stopped to say –

'Come on, if you'd be happy do what I'm doing. There's nothing wrong with singing and dancing. Let's make every street our dance floor.'

Starved for such excitement all these years, this last call from Dolly was enough to drive them mad. The rich or poor, young or old, male or female – everyone's heart was captured magnetically. Even the shyest mothers could not hold themselves back and joined her, in cheery carelessness, to grab the opportunity, with both hands.

The tranquil town was shaking under the dainty feet of the dancing beauty. She was the first and only girl, who had ever dared to stir the serenity of Chandigarh.

I stared in awe, when Dolly sprung a surprise, by changing her dancing style from Flash to Disco – arms flying and feet stomping to a swift, vigorous rhythm. That incited the boys to pat her hips and she bounced like an ethereally intoxicated *apsara*: but at that moment she did not care, as the drunkenness of the dance had transfigured her into a self-forgetful *fille de joie.* This created an ugly and reptilious impression, on some high-up moralist, in the crowd.

'Stop this crude, open air show!' The high-up moralist shouted, but his shout was a whisper, compared to the noise of the crowd. So it didn't get what the 80-year-old die-hard had expected. He was now boiling with anger. When his anger was almost at breaking point, he swore *'Kalyug hai, kalyug'* and left the scene, in utter disgust.

Soon after, the departing moralist's influence resurfaced on two idealists in their mid-sixties, a devoted pair, standing close together. They were conversing in a low, clear voice.

'From the look of things, she is out to upset the town.'

'I'd say she is corrupting the young minds.'

'Rather, she is out to win the hearts of Chandigarhians,' a college chick behind me, shouted them down.

'You speak of winning, *Yaar*,' thumping him on the back, his friend fomented, 'She has already won us. She is the Queen of Hearts.'

'There's no doubt about it,' a pretty girl chipped in. 'Never was such a crowd seen before in the history of Chandigarh.' The girl's excited face spread in a delighted grin.

That provoked another senior townsman to condemn Dolly openly:

'She is the Queen of Devils, she is amoral; she is a free woman.'

'She is not a free woman,' someone refuted, at the top of his voice. 'She is free spirit, a man's heart-throb and a woman's pride.'

'And she has the fairest face that has ever graced our dull town,' a merry voice further irritated them.

'Shame! Shame! She is a blot on our Chandigarh.' Then, in hurried whisper the stubborn duo, still clinging to a bygone era, swore, 'We're not going to allow this crude, open air show.'

A collegian in a faded blue shirt retorted, 'That's what you can only think of. To most men of your age the charm of living is a thing of the past.'

'Sheer lack of vision.' added a squeaky voice. 'Their dim eyes cannot see the changes taking place in life's pattern, throughout the world.'

'Indeed, son, it is too bad on our part not to be able to see what you see. But we're ashamed of seeing a Bitch-Goddess trampling the peace and order of our daily life.'

'Bitch Goddess – that's a laugh! She is the Love-Goddess from heaven, to whip life into this lifeless town.'

During the encounter a spoiled youngster poked fun, 'See! See! Grandpa, see! Your dead yesterdays are coming alive,' and everyone within listening range laughed.

Of the two, the bespectacled idealist, made another futile attempt at injecting a sense of morality:

'Dancing in the streets shamelessly is no pleasant sight, my son. Nor is it good for our society.'

'Don't criticise what you don't understand.' Timing it, a rough voice fired.

Both the idealists fumed in rage. 'You stupid rascal.'

'Huh! A little excitement for a change. What's bad about it?' Queried a wag.

'Nothing! Nothing at all! Chandigarh can go to hell for all you care.'

I looked at scholarly collegian, who stood near him and said politely:

'Grandpa, you resent this, because people like you sentimentalise the past and prevent the young ones from going forward.'

'You are mistaken, son. This is nothing but going backward rather than forward.'

'I can't stand street dances.' The other idealist gave vent to his disturbed mind. 'Can nothing be done?' He spoke into his ear.

'There is only one way to stop this nuisance.'

'Ah Grandpa, don't be a killjoy!' A loose-tongue, in the crowd flapped.

'It will be wrong on our part if we allow the street dancers to go unpunished.' Both the idealists now conspired in an undertone.

'As if these two, old fools are the guardians of public morality,' remarked a strangely, bold girl.

Another daring teenager, with all the arrogance of youth, challenged them, 'Dear sirs of the older generation, why waste all that time? Do what you like.'

'Huh! Who's afraid of old fools?' Scoffed an athletically built young man

The errant's unwarranted tongue infuriated the old men, and they left hastily, plotting vengeance. Obviously, it was police action, an extreme step, that they went to seek.

In our country *'lathi-charge'* is a common device for dispersing a mob, political or non-political. Terrified by the coming danger, I kept looking out for the armoured police vans.

Then, to climax things, they came sooner than I thought, weaving through the crowd. The closed doors of the vans suddenly burst open, in the middle of the main square. Giving no warning, the hefty *law-and-orderwallahs* fell upon the gay townsmen, like hungry hawks.

For some moments the confusion reigned supreme over the gaiety. Then it was a stampede. The shocked townsmen ran for shelter, yelling and screaming.

I knew what would come next – arrest.

'Dolly!' I called out.

The urgency in my tone made her look sharply.

'Trouble?'

'Don't ask. Run before it is too late. We're in for serious trouble.'

She realised the turn of the situation and needed no urging.

Seventeen

We were running for safety.

'What's happening?' Dolly asked, shaken.

'Police.'

'Police? Why?'

'To arrest the Bombay girl.'

'But everyone was dancing. Why should the police single me out?'

'The target is always the ringleader.'

'Of all people are you blaming me, Sanchu?'

'Because no other girl was exhibiting herself like you.'

'Didn't I conquer danger through song and dance?'

'Huh, conquered! Rather, you got us all into hot water.'

'My good man, at that awkward moment, modesty through arguments or reason, was impossible.'

'That doesn't mean one should shake off decency.'

'I know, but that was a case where urgency over-rode decency.'

'Under no circumstances should a girl be so demonstrative.'

Dolly's face became very red. She retaliated,

'What did I demonstrate? Did I take off my clothes?'

'Dolly, let's not indulge in quarrelling. You know, in a woman, man looks for three things – modesty, femininity and fidelity.'

'I didn't ask men to come after me. Did I?'

'When girls show what they have, what choice do men have?' I cut her argument to ribbons.

Pride demolished, Dolly's face turned pale and she became a lot humbler.

'No one has ever told me all this, till now.'

It was like a blind girl, who was suddenly able to see.

'Now that you've understood what I mean, please, for God's sake, cut out this nonsensical argument and keep running.'

She didn't need further scolding. Sensing the danger, she buttoned up her lips and quickened her pace.

So busy were the policemen in dispersing the crowd, that they did not even know when and how we bamboozled them and took to the Link Road.

No more than ten minutes of silent running than she gave up, clinging to my sleeve.

'Don't hold me like that. Relax,' I said, halting.

'I...I...'

She was too exhausted and could barely find her words.

In this safer zone, we felt relieved but the fear of the police did not leave us. With slow, easy strides, we were now pushing off, knowing where to go next – the Yatch Club.

'It's your timely warning that saved me from landing in jail.' She showed two rows perfect teeth, a reward of merit that I didn't accept.

'Just keep on walking. I'm not asking for testimonials.'

Given a little deliverance, she would at once ride on your shoulder.

Away from the maddening crowd, we were walking down a solitary avenue. When we came upon a block of flats, I saw an old couple sitting in the balcony, close to each other.

The man had an Alsatian dog at his feet whom he patted every now and then, while the woman read out poems, from a slender book of poetry There was a calm expression on her face, a faint smile played on her lips.

In the quiet noon, their closeness looked highly symbolic of true companionship, keeping romance alive.

My companion raised her eyebrows, flashed a smile at me and then suddenly, her face turned crimson.

Not a single soul was on the road, a car honked from the distant rear. As it came closer, Dolly waved her hand expecting it to stop. But the pleasant looking, young man, driving the car swept past us without a glance. Dolly glared after the car and cursed: 'Devil! I wish the car goes out of order.'

In consequence, the car stopped with a groan, just two hundred yards away from us, as homage to her wish.

'Look-look-look!' I nudged her in the ribs. 'It's a breakdown.'

'That's as it should be!' Dolly threw her arms up in delight. 'Very good. Very, very good. It serves him right,' yelling, she leapt into the air.

In her wild excitement, she stamped my right foot.

'Ouch! Dolly, stop kicking; it hurts!'

'Oh, I'm sorry!'

'You should be!'

She was immediately apologetic.

'Now look, what you've done to my sandal!' I voiced my agony, showing her the snapped-off strap. 'Where will I find a cobbler in this forsaken place?'

'Good grief!' She muttered to herself. Then, standing on tiptoe, she made a quick spot survey of the place. 'That's him.' Pointing at the turbaned head, not very far away, she exclaimed, 'The surgeon of shoes!'

A middle-aged man, surrounded by an array of tools and heaps of old shoes, in various stages of surgery, was hammering away on his anvil, sitting near the telephone booth, on the street corner.

'Ah, what eyes' I said admiringly.

At once she drew a long face. 'What's wrong with my nose, Sanchu?'

'Nothing. Why?'

'You should know, girls don't like their eyes praised and nose neglected.'

That slit of her eyes told me what she wanted and reacting promptly I ran a caressing finger over her nose bridge. 'I doubt if even Miss Universe has as beautiful a nose as yours.'

'Thank you,' she mumbled bashfully.

'Now, if you'll excuse me, I'll get my sandal mended.'

'Right. You get your sandal fixed, I'll see what's ailing the driver.'

'Okay.'

And presently, we both went in opposite directions.

In no time the cobbler mended my sandal. Running and walking, I tried to catch up with Dolly but she was then, within a few yards of the car.

The bonnet of the car was open. I could see a man was peering at the engine.

'Can I help you?' Dolly called when I was within earshot.

The displeased motorist looked up sharply.

'I doubt it,' he said, making no effort to conceal his bad temper.

'Let me have a look,' she said and bent over the hot engine. 'What were the symptoms?'

'The damned thing gave a splutter and packed up.'

'All right for petrol?'

'The tank's full. The blasted thing's always going wrong.'

'It's probably carburettor trouble. Got any tools?'

'You know, this is pretty decent of you.' The motorist opened the glove compartment and took out a small, canvas, tool kit. As Dolly took it from his hand, he asked, 'Where is your husband?'

'Here,' I said appearing from behind. 'My wife is very clever with her hands. I'm sure she can put your carburettor on its feet again.'

'That's fine.' Unimpressed, the motorist looked doubtfully at Dolly, who was then busy dismantling the carburettor. 'Talk about good Samaritans,' he said and added with a smile, 'I don't know a thing about cars.'

'Well, it's our luck, too,' I said. 'We lost our way and were looking for a lift.'

A wide grin creased the motorist's face. 'May be my car broke down only for giving you a lift.'

Dolly looked up, showing all her teeth in the smile, then became serious again, with the carburettor.

While she took down the carburettor, the motorist made himself agreeable to her. He seemed almost regretful when she reassembled the carburettor, adjusted the last screw and told him to start the engine.

'I think she'll start now,' she said loftily. 'The feed was blocked by the look of it. Anyway, try her.'

The engine fired, at the first touch of the starter.

'You really are a marvel.' He said, beaming out of the car window. 'Well, hop in, the two of you. Where can I drop you?'

'We're going to the Yacht Club,' Dolly said excitedly. 'You couldn't drop us there, could you?'

'Why not? I'd be glad to. It's on my way,' said the motorist, opening the car door.

A lift we desired; yet, unsure of his behaviour, we hesitated unmoving.

'Don't blink. Don't fear either. I'm a gentleman.' The motorist assured us, with a sunny smile.

Yielding to necessity, we got in.

Driving in silence for some time, the motorist, who was all too eager to chat, asked, 'You're out on your honeymoon, eh?'

'No sir, we're on our way to find happiness,' replied Dolly, tossing an exaggerated comic wink at me.

'Right choice. The Sukhna Lake, honeymooners' paradise, holds all the happiness in the world.' Humouring us with a smile, he slowed down the car and turned off the main road, onto a secondary road. Stopping the car at the right place, he indicated a box-shaped sign.

'Just there.'

Following the pointing finger, my eyes found a big sign that spelt in red and yellow lettering: YACHT CLUB.

The arrow under the sign pointed to a gravel path, leading to the gate. 'Well…' the motorist held out a friendly hand.

'Thanks for the ride.' I shook his hand warmly and got out of the car.

'Thank your wife. She alone could make this tin-pot run.' He grinned at Dolly who was already on the footpath. 'So long… have sun and fun,' triggering his parting shot, the motorist drove away.

We started walking along the gravel path flanked on both sides by trimmed lawns and flowerbeds. Dolly confided:

'I think the Creator has made us for each other.'

The fanciful idea, seemingly childish, struck no answering spark.

She continued, 'You must have noticed, everywhere we are mistaken as a honeymoon couple.'

Giving no sign of hearing, I walked on, with a sad Dolly at my side.

Outside the gate, we paused.

'Hello, lucky pair!' A young member of the Yacht Club, just returning after boating, greeted us and before I could accost him, was off on his motorcycle.

'Hi hi hi...'

Dolly's rippling 'hi hi hi's' had caused several heads to turn towards her.

'Please hold all your 'hi hi hi's' inside.'

'But I can't.' Vainly striving to control herself, only she let out a great, belly laugh again.

At this point, the smiling gatekeeper waved us in, through the gate.

Eighteen

On the outskirts of Chandigarh, in splendid isolation, lies the Sukhna Lake, like a broad road of water, curving distantly. Upon the lake, our boat was floating like a swan on blue waters. In romantic twosome, another boat drifted past us and vanished around the bend.

'That's 'Leila.' What's the name of our boat, Sanchu?' Dolly asked.

'Sagar Kanya.'

'Sagar Kanya?' She echoed.

'Meaning daughter of the ocean.'

'Have all our oceans dried up, Sanchu?'

'What an absurd question! Has any ocean dried up anywhere?'

'Then I'm right. This boat is wrongly named.'

'Well, if you look at the name cynically, you're never at a loss to criticise it.'

'But the ignorance of the difference between ocean and lake, is inexcusable. I am going to mention this romantic illogic in the Visitors' Book.'

'Well, what's in a name?'

'What do you mean by quoting Shakespeare?'

'I mean, there's nothing in a name.'

'Lots in a name. Shouldn't a name have some meaning, some background, some harmony?'

'Now Dolly, you're making something big, out of nothing.'

'But a name with no real substance, no relevance to logic and no respect for one's noble heritage is likely to create confusion. You're not trying to understand.'

'But why waste energy on such silly arguments? After all, a boat is a boat. With any name it will float.'

The phraseology welled up a bubbling laugh, forcing the topic to drop.

Dolly had sat in the stern, with her feet together. Her left hand rested on the side of the boat and the right shaded her eyes from the fierce, midday sun. Her hair was piled high, to prevent the breeze from playing tricks with it.

The freshened air had the odour of the lake and of wet earth, and the lake had a most expressive feature, of its own. It animated and enlivened the whole scene. A line of forest clad hills, walled the deep blue waters of the calm lake. Having feasted her eyes on the untamed beauty of the hills, Dolly drew in her breath sharply, then let it out slowly, in a sign of sheer enchantment.

While she was far too absorbed in her surroundings, I was stabbing the water, with slow oars, on the breast of the greenish blue lake.

Consequently, a profound, philosophical realisation about the scenery, dawned on me. That the lake and the hill had once lived together.

Just as the parting of the soul leaves a body lifeless, similarly, the lake, the soul of the hill, flowed down and left the hill a dumb onlooker. From then on, the winged messengers of the voiceless hill, sing of their reunion from the tree-tops, while the grazing cows hold swing their tails in calm indifference. The hill does not know that the lake holds its mirrored reflection, just as a human being on to yesterday.

A short while, after the wind roared in my ears and all at once, the philosophical thought was snapped.

Back to myself I was trying to spot the other boats, spread out upon the waters here and there; away from those out of sight, near the left bank after the bend, I grounded our boat.

Dolly craned her neck in all directions, filling her eyes with the spectacular view the unique place offered. 'Beautiful! A sight I shall never forget!' She beamed, resting her wandering eyes on me. 'What's now, Sanchu?'

Raising the oars and laying them up along the sides of the boat, I replied, 'For now, this boat is here to stay. Let's change into swimming costumes before the other boats arrive.'

'How can I change in front of you?'

'Shy?'

'Don't be silly.' Dolly smiled one of her quick, girlish smiles. 'If ever I were, would I have come with you, all this distance?'

'Thank you for coming.' I smiled back at her, making a small bow.

There was a long moment of nothing. Then Dolly asked, 'Can't we go to the shore, Sanchu?'

'You'll have to wade.'

'Why don't you carry me?' She suggested, like a love-hungry, little girl.

Not reacting to Dolly's suggestion, I rolled up my slacks to my knees. I took off my sandals and left them in the boat. Steeping out into the glassy water as I made for the shore, I heard.

'Now who is shy?'

I stopped. Sharply turning, I asked, 'Is that a challenge?'

Just wordless and quiet, holding out her arms wide, she was standing, a smiling siren.

'Okay.' Wading back a few steps, first I twirled her around then scooped her up in the air.

Feeling wildly adventurous, she said, 'Sanchu, I enjoy being with you.'

'Any girl would.'

'Oh, it's fantastic! Romantic! Exotic!'

She was thrilled the way I carried her. I enjoyed it, because she wasn't heavy. And the moment I planted her feet onto the lake bank, she giggled away into the nearby wood where the head-high *sarkanda* grass, afforded adequate cover.

Behind a bush I changed into striped, swimming trunks. While waiting for Dolly, my wandering eyes stumbled on a pair of ground squirrels, fighting over the turf that would become a winter home, for mate and offspring. Chirping madly, the rivals dashed at each other, tails raised. The battle was fierce but short; the loser scuttled off humiliated. The victor preened, standing on hind legs, surveying a domain, where shoots of giant grass had began to sprout. It was about that time Dolly came out of the wood in a strapless swimsuit, bubbling with excitement.

'I can race you across,' she challenged from hearing distance.

'I know you can,' I said nodding in agreement.

The challenger was now coming with considerable speed. Suddenly, stumbling to a halt, she looked upward, directly at me.

'Are you hurt?' I asked with concern.

'No,' replied Dolly with emphasis, trying to hide the pain.

Even so, I felt sorry and looked away.

A few seconds later, she came unhurriedly and stopped beside me. And then, regarding me from more angles than a geometry book has, she began to examine my body clinically, somewhat in the style of an Army Medical Officer.

'Oh dear! Does this mean I'm under inspection?'

'Very much so.' Dolly, looking very serious, continued with her most intense scrutiny.

'Okay. Okay.' Faintly embarrassed, I switched my attention to the occupants of a passing boat.

'You've a perfect body.' She paid the greatest compliment of my life, adding, 'I like smooth muscles.'

'I'm flattered.'

'No, Sanchu, no! I'm not flattering. You do have an excellent physique, athletically built. You've all the qualities a real man should have.'

'My mother'd kill you if she ever heard you cataloguing my physical charms.'

'And your father?'

The reference to my father had an inexplicable effect on me, making it impossible to hold back the tears that had begun filling my eyes.

'My father! That kind and friendly, old man, he's my ideal of how a father should direct his son.' Oddly enough, my mind raced back four years, to the unforgettable night.

Around 12 o'clock of the unforgettable night, cutting all sentimental bonds, as I steeped out of my sleepy, village home, my father's deep voice immobilised me.

'Well, son, the first hour after midnight has always been the best hour to run away from home, when the rest of the family members are fast asleep.'

Before I could come up with a plausible excuse, I felt his gentle hands on my shoulders.

'Papa.'

'I am not stopping you. I guess you have to do what's right for you and must act as your instincts guide.' He surprised me by saying. 'I myself had wanted to be a writer but...' his voice strangled with emotion. Pausing, he continued, 'A writer needs to be alone to write well. A quiet place is the only solution. And how much the want of the right environment affects creative work, I understand. That's why, one has to give up something to gain something. That was a risk I couldn't take, because of my early marriage.'

'For choosing to become a writer, a difficult occupation, you will have to sweat and struggle a lot. You'll find the challenge daunting, I warn you. The hurdles, many; The hours long; But then, a decision is a decision; you just can't turn off and on from this to that. So, you have to be optimistic. And don't you ever forget it, comforts and pleasure are not on the cards of a struggling writer. Lastly, desire for intimacy with a woman must be avoided, at all costs.

'Of late, led by a premonition of a moment such as this, I had been regularly putting some money for you under my bed.' His hands still held on my shoulders, he smiled. 'All I can offer you is a few hundred rupees,' and he shoved a small packet into my hand.

His words inspired new courage. In profound gratitude, respect and love, as I bowed to touch his feet, he threw both arms around me and kissed my cheek, one last time.

Many silent moments passed. Not a word was spoken. In the end, with a note of fear in his tone, he said, 'Well, son... you'll keep contact. Won't you?'

'Oh, Papa!' Bursting into tears, I clung to him. 'How can I say goodbye to you?'

Back in the present, I heard Dolly say: 'You haven't answered my question.'

'For the answer... you might have to meet my father.'

'You father's son!' She aimed a mocking jab at my ribs. Then, grabbing me by the arm, she towed me down to the water's edge. There, in ankle deep water, we stood poised for a few seconds, trying to fathom the depth of the lake.

Hardly able to contain her excitement, Dolly gamely pulled me. 'Aw, come on.'

'Don't pull, unless you have a hidden wish to drown me.'

Dolly's eyebrows raised. 'What, you don't know swimming?'

It was more of a statement than a question.

'I didn't say it, but are you a good swimmer?'

'Better than many,' she replied, adding, 'A fact, not a boast.'

'Despite your being a good swimmer, which I don't doubt, we shall swim closer to shore, for safety's sake. You know, it's better to be safe than sorry.'

'You're overcautious,' she smiled. Then, with a naughty glint in her eyes, she asked, 'Anything else?'

'And you'll stay close to me.'

'Don't worry – like glue.'

And finally, we dived into the warm water together.

But before the ripple reached the distant shores, I resurfaced to see if she was really a good swimmer. I saw her approaching me, churning the blue water with fish-like ease, the large eyes dilated, the lips parted, her long hair trailing...

Seized by some childish desire, as I caught her trailing hair playfully, she turned on me with a big splash. Then came the typical reaction – with her arms firmly around my waist, she pulled me hard against her and began kissing me, greedily.

When, afterwards, the reality washed over me, unhurried, she was floating away semi-submerged, blissfully undulating her body like a water nymph.

A moral dilemma niggled at a corner of my mind: 'Should I? Or shouldn't I?' But I shunned the word 'moral', preferring 'vengeance', since the moralist in me had gone into temporary hibernation. With, the kiss still stuck in my mouth, I went madly after her, to settle scores.

Reaching her with a few fast strokes as I caught her leg, she slipped away, like a slippery eel. After several near misses I succeeded in grabbing her armpits. Then I pinned her to the lake floor, with all my strength. Thus overpowered, she lay on her back almost paralysed in fear, for she thought her virginity was at stake. Came and went a second's hesitation before I kissed her, long and hard, but that was as far as I went.

Immediately after the score was settled, I freed her. She, with one deft, body movement, moved away swiftly. Then her head pushing upwards, her feet paddling, she began knifing the water fiercely. By the time her head broke the water surface, I was standing in neck-deep water, watching her movements.

Filling the lungs with oxygen, soon she revitalised herself and her attacks began. Again and again, and again. Somehow, I foiled all her attempts by dodging, or pushing her away, but without hurting her. Baffled, she finally gave up saying – 'I know what you are.'

'Sorry Dolly, only emotional harassment drove me to take such an extreme step.'

'Or a temptation which you couldn't resist?'

'No sense in asking this now.'

'Nevertheless, to put it plainly, you're a very sexy man beneath your elegant, cultured exterior.'

'Dolly, please stop agonising me.'

'The truth is not palatable.

Dolly's slyly cool, satirical tone outraged me. 'The real truth is that women are the sexier lot. They make love to anyone they fancy. And any time.'

'Are you speaking from experience?'

'What rubbish! Never before in my life, except for you, have I been so close to any woman, that I should have some experience.'

'Really you're an interesting creature,' she mumbled.

The words were only a whisper and I could hardly hear it.

'Pardon?'

'Nothing,' she shrugged off. 'Anyway, with little a coaching and coaxing, you'll make quite an acceptable lover,' she whispered huskily.

'I don't know what had got into me...' I muttered, more to myself than to her.

'Retaliation was not entirely unexpected. That the cool cucumber would turn into a hot potato, I just can't believe it.'

'I must confess I crossed the limit.'

'Hardly.'

'Aren't you angry?'

'Nonsense!' She laughed out loud. 'On the contrary, I'm delighted.'

'Thank you, God!' I breathed a sigh of relief.

'Now that we've tasted the nectar – lets splash around for a few, more pleasant minutes.'

'Please don't harass me with your naughty suggestion.'

'Come on now, Sanchu; don't shy away from reality.'

'Once was enough. Not again. Understand?'

'No. I don't care to understand a man, who always keeps a tight rein on his emotions.'

'One has to, if he has a goal.'

'Goal needn't be the sole criterion of life.'

'What else then, should it be?'

Just then, out of the blue, there on the shore, two men appeared. The one, a little ahead of the other, came and stood with his feet almost touching the water; the other halted two paces behind him. Like statues, unmoving and silent, their unblinking marble eyes were firmly set on Dolly's bare neck, who was then standing in shoulder-deep water, with her back to them.

Feeling a burning sensation on the neck, a purely female intuition (God's gift to woman), Dolly turned round, to meet the two, queer-looking men. All this time she was not aware of their menacing presence. Although scared she shouted at them with enormous authority in her voice:

'You shameless oglers, what business have you here?'

'Beg your pardon, madam, would you like to be rescued?'

'Who the hell are you?' Dolly thundered.

The two obnoxious men, standing stiffly to attention, speaking almost in union, answered her, 'We're Lifeguards from Yacht Club.'

That cooled Dolly's temper subtly.

'Thank you for coming. Please leave us alone. We can take care of ourselves.'

They were already regretting their humble offer of voluntary help. Now, between themselves, they conversed in a very low voice.

'Junior…'

'Yes, senior.'

'She seems to be a minister's daughter.'

'Could be.'

'You two devils! What's holding you up now?' Dolly censured.

'Why is her temper so short-fused?' asked the junior.

'That's her status symbol?' replied the senior.

'I scent trouble. Do you?'

'Yes. I do'

'Now what'd we do?'

'We'll run at once.'

And they fled, like released animals.

Once again, just Dolly and me, alone.

'So what have you decided?' asked Dolly. 'Splashing around for a few pleasant minutes or…'

'Why not? Especially when the request is from such a lovely young woman who belongs to half the nation's population?'

'Enough is enough.' And she gave a hard pull, that broke the shell of my shyness.

Soon we were thrashing round in circles. Then begun the chasing game, across the lake, more like a merry-go-round.

When at last the spell of swimming ended, the few pleasant minutes had stretched to an hour. Exhausted, almost beyond endurance, somehow steadying ourselves, we got out of the lake clinging to each other. Then, walking like zombies, we made for the shore, until we collapsed in a tumbling heap, a little away from the water's edge.

And everything was suddenly very quiet.

Nineteen

Seconds and minutes went by, breezily.

It was much later when I awoke, opened my eyes and smiled lazily at the sky. The parting sun was then hanging above the hill for a last, loving longing look at the earth. It was a fond farewell.

As the sun swooped down the hill, the various shades of crimson, mauve, magenta and purple, played a quick game of hide-and-seek, giving repeated hints that silent darkness was fast approaching.

The beautiful evening, with sailing boats on the lake and the horizon merging into infinity, lured the twilight radiance to linger on. The creeping silence lent importance to the hooting of the owls, in harmony with the lazy chopping of oars.

For a long while, I lay awake on my back, staring at the sky. Dolly was lying beside me, with her breath warming my shoulder, unconscious of her sex.

'So beautiful, and so near!' I said to myself and closed my eyes. Cupidity breathed from my every pore, and in imagination I wrapped myself in her hair. I pressed myself between her breasts to suffer a divine suffocation; I longed to put my arms around her, to pull her closer to me, smother her with kisses. But fear mounted in me that she might not yield; she might even feel indignant, shocked, angry, disgusted and even slap me, or might scream for help. She might run away from me forever, because I had misinterpreted a friendly gesture and then, of course, I would be left standing here on the lakeside, stammering apologies, and the sky would fall, all my dreams would shatter and come crashing down, like broken glass, around my feet.

Frozen by these thoughts for minutes, I rolled over on my side, facing her, cautiously enough, to make it look like a casual sleepy gesture.

I saw my companion's beautiful face plastered with wet hair and the rosebud lushness of those slightly parted lips, the cute curve of her nose, of her pointed chin. She was looking so strangely serene at that moment that I could not take my eyes off. Apart from the bathing costume, her body was garmentless. Her eyes were closed as if in sleep. Her travel-tired limbs, stretched out on the green, contrasted pleasantly with her milky complexion. Her perfectly formed breasts, that guarded her heart and its secret were rising and falling with her breath. She was not aware that her left breast had spilled out silkily from her bodice and the coral pink nipple had popped out.

I stole a look at it.

Then, in a sudden shyness, her hands went to shield her breasts.

Abashed, I averted my gaze but my conscience pronounced me guilty.

'Mud in your eyes.' Sitting up, she spat out with scorn, grabbed her towel, wrapped herself and walked away into the wood where lay her cast-off clothes, her body erect, proud and contemptuous.

Filled with self-reproach, I told myself 'You'd better get dressed before she's back,' and hurried off to the mango tree where I had discarded my clothes. Putting them on, I waited for Dolly to come. It was uncanny how, at times, Dolly seemed to know my thoughts. I did not know how I was expected to act.

Some minutes later, her face appeared above the shoulder-high giant grasses; she was coming, towelling her hair.

I waited praying; *Please God, don't make her reopen my guilt.*

She came.

I hoped now she would speak and at that precise moment, I heard her low voice.

'Coward!'

Accusation, reproach, hatred and shock, were all in that one word. Ridden with guilt, I passed my tongue nervously over my lips.

'I thought you would say something like that.'

'Cowardice is a sign of inferiority.'

'All right then, I'm inferior.'

'Do you think we can get along with this kind of inferiority?'

'You're quite right, but what have I done?'

'Do I have to tell you?'

'Honestly, I can't make head or tail of it.'

'Don't try playing Mr Innocent with me. It won't work.'

I wondered: *How did she come to know?*

'If you're thinking how I knew...' said Dolly, breaking in upon my thoughts.

Startled I asked, 'How did you know?'

'It's just the sort of thing a woman knows instinctively.'

Dolly's eyes were fixed upon me and I did not want to meet them, remembering the look I had stolen and which had left me ashamed and troubled. Keeping my gaze on the distant hill, I mumbled a mute apology.

'Muteness is a trick of the offender, devised to conceal the guilt. But it cannot liquefy the guilt into innocence.'

Unexpectedly, my own anger grew and I reacted strongly, to Dolly's utterance.

'And just what do you expect as a penalty? Must I tear out my eyes and place them at your feet?'

'Still it won't be enough.'

'Wonderful! When I plucked you bodily from the water and carried you in my arms, were you dead?'

'It was merely a play, without physical attention.'

'In that case, I'm just beginning to learn what morality is.'

'It is concerned with how we behave towards each other, not with how much of our bodies we happen to display.'

'May be you're right. But are you not confusing desire with passion?'

'There can be no desire without passion. It's something like the reflection of the tree in the lake; it couldn't exist without the tree.'

'But I'll not admit that desire is passion. Desire is the natural phenomenon of the sexual instinct, while passion is destructive and thrives on impediment.'

'Sanchu, you often think you know a great deal more than you actually do,' Dolly said acidly.

My monumental patience crumbled at last and I hit back at her, most indecorously.

'Doesn't matter. It is natural with every man to look at things worth seeing.'

'Bah! Have you no shame, to speak like this?'

'How could I be other than worldly?'

Casting a sour look, she countered, 'Why, then, do you so often speak like a saint?'

'Do I, really? I don't know.'

'Sanchu, pretension is not conducive to any useful solution.'

'Rubbish! Let's cut out this nonsense, Dolly, okay?'

'Okay. Just see that it does not happen again.'

'All right. It won't.'

'Okay then.' Dolly's face alighted with forgiveness and love, dispelling the gloom.

For some minutes, no words passed between us. Shaking out her soaked hair, she said at length, 'My hair keeps falling down.'

'Because it's wet.'

'I don't know what to do with it,' she said and furiously pushed it back.

Her hair was annoying her, as it constantly escaped from the knot and fell on her eyes.

'It's such a nuisance, I feel like cutting it off.'

'Don't say that. Long hair personifies beauty.'

'If it is so, why don't you grow long hair?'

'The hippies are good specimens. In recent years, they have reshaped many male heads around the world.'

'Oh you! She pushed me unawares and ran off. 'Here I go.'

Her behaviour was always unpredictable. However, I narrowly escaped from falling. I saw her running, with her long hair flopping at her back.

'Catch me if you can.' Halting, she challenged me to a race.

'I can, if I want to,' I said aloud. 'You are challenging a fast runner.'

'Prove it.'

The game pleased me and I accepted; but I wanted to spur her interest by a wager.

'The one who loses,' I said, 'Will be obliged to do whatever the victor wishes.'

'Agreed,' she said and sprinted away.

Seeing that she did not run very fast, I was sure of winning; but wanted to lose, in order to see what she would compel me to do. She was running with all her might, while I held myself in check, falling behind her gradually.

On reaching the edge of the lake where our boat was anchored, the thrill of the game ended.

'You're the victor,' I declared, clapping.

'And the fastest runner is a mere boaster,' Dolly said, with the elan of a victor.

'Defeat is a wiser choice than victory when the opponent is a beautiful girl like you.'

'I must say, that's a nice way of not admitting defeat.'

'Never! I didn't mean so. I do admit, I've lost. What's your wish? I'll obey.'

'I wish you don't ever look at me in that evil way again.'

The words 'evil way' sounded dreadful. I bowed to her wish. Then, silently, we waded back to the boat.

As before, Dolly sat at the stern. I pushed the boat off and scrambled aboard. The boat swayed and rushed forward. Then, shaking herself, she quickly levelled her head towards the Yacht Club. The oar in my hands chopped and jagged at the water.

Dolly, leaning on her side, dipped a hand into the cold water, and let it trail, feeling the light rippling pull at her wrist. But every now and then she was eyeing me sideways. Sitting ramrod straight, I rowed on and on, as I no longer had the courage to look at her.

At last she asked, what was on my mind.

'What's there to be depressed about, my dear Mr Innocent?'

Thinking that silence would be wisest, I made no reply.

'To be a little weak, instead of being strong all the time, is not at all a bad thing,' she herself reasoned out, in an attempt to bridge the gap between us. 'In any case, you don" have to feel guilty.'

'You mean it, Dolly? Honestly?'

'Why, sure! We all have our weaknesses, don't you think?' I nodded agreement and she continued, 'There're examples where even *Mahatmas* had no control over themselves. After all, a man is a man and you know as well I do, that no man is without some weakness.'

Inspite of all her comfortable reason I lowered my head, feeling guilty. The stigma stuck deep in my heart and I dared not look at her.

As though in acceptance of my repentance, there came floating in the air, a captivating voice, accompanied by honey-sweet strains from a harmonium. I listened. The familiar tune, taken from a good classical *raga,* enthralled me. Still clearer and clearer... it took the shape of a devotional song. Quite coincidentally, it happened to be my favourite song. The music washed my soul and the appeal in the song helped me regain my peace of mind.

For a second, I looked at Dolly, who was watching the golden waters, her eyes without a trace of fear, a fear that perhaps grips every young woman, in the company of a young man, with the falling of darkness. So fearless and unselfconscious, she matched both in character and physique, like an Indian girl, and yet so unlike one, she could totally engross or ignore my existence.

Twenty

Night has already lowered her curtain of black velvet.

With a million stars above our heads we stood outside the Yacht Club, looking for a taxi. Cars, mobikes and scooters were just parked about, higgledy-piggledy, everywhere. But no taxi could be seen anywhere. Hoping to find ourselves one, we started for the main road. Presently, Dolly said:

'I'm hungry as a hog.'

'And I'm tired as a dog,' I parodied.

'Fooling me, Sanchu?'

'No,' I said, smiling. 'Outwitting.'

'Honestly, Sanchu, I'm very hungry.'

'That's very unfair on your part.'

'What's so unfair about it?'

'When I'm faced with a problem, you glutton, can think only of food for your tummy.'

I was prepared to accept her reprimand had she spluttered one – instead she whined in a wounded voice: 'I can't help it if I am an addict to food, can I?'

Could I, after that, further hurt her? Therefore, I said nothing. When we reached the main road, we stopped. On the footpath we stood in silence, looking for a taxi. We waited longer than five minutes, longer than ten, longer than fifteen, but none came.

Taxis, during the night, were rare in this lonely part of Chandigarh but cars kept swishing by, ignoring our misery. Dolly looked at the sky, seeking God's mercy for a cab. The silence went stretching through, second after second. When she received no answer from God, she exploded:

'This then, is your goddamn Chandigarh, the pride of India!'

Hunger and anger are easy partners, I wanted to say. But not wanting to be cruelly truthful, I chose to keep silent.

The night was cool and clear. Not a soul was in sight excepting us. A gusty wind rattled the poster frames, loosely clamped on the lamp posts. I lit cigarette and flicked the match away, eyed my companion sympathetically and blew a long cloud of cigarette smoke.

An empty taxi came by some freak chance, bringing at last, the end to the long wait. We waved to it and jumped in. As I slammed the door shut, the hungry hog commanded:

'Drive us to a hotel that serves the best Punjabi dishes.'

'Excuse me *Memsaab*, no hotel will serve meals tonight.'

'What a wretched place, this Chandigarh!'

'Not inhospitable to its visitors.' Our turbaned cabby bloated with pride, in defence of his birthplace. Then, as if anticipating another bitter remark from Dolly, he added hastily, 'Normally, it is not so cut-and-dry.'

'Bullshit!' The haughty, naughty, beauty hurled the foul word, in profound disgust.

Upset, *Sardar Sahib* got very red in the face.

'Good God, Dolly! Ladies don't use that kind of language.'

'I warn you, Sanchu, please keep out of this.'

In the uneasy calm that ensued, I was dying to ask *Sardarji* why the hotels wouldn't serve meals and the question tripped off my tongue:

'Are the hotels on strike?'

No answer.

'Is someone important dead?'

Again no answer.

'Any mishap?'

Still no answer. Only his face hardened, while his eyes continued to stare fixedly beyond, at the windshield.

'Something terrible must have happened? What?'

My gentle persuasion worked.

He now turned on me, in a swift movement. For one tense moment, he eyed me with suspicion. Then, adjusting his turban at a jaunty angle, he favoured me with the answer.

'This evening, the President of the Chandigarh Hotels' Association died, in a car accident.'

'I'm sorry,' I said sincerely.

'You do understand, sir, how unfortunate this is?'

'I do understand,' I said, in a consoling voice.

'And there is a town-wide, general shutdown of hotels to mark the passing away, is it?' Dolly was unreasonably rude and I was inexpressibly ashamed.

'Only for tonight.' His voice was quiet, low and sad.

'Starving us, his soul shall not be in peace,' she cursed, breaking all the rules of decency.

'The human element is very important, Dolly. That's the trouble with you. You have no sense of the human element at all.'

'We're talking about hotels of Chandigarh, Sanchu.'

'Yes, of course, but still, you haven't any sense of the human element.'

'No I haven't.'

Poor hungry devil! Her brain was dead with hunger. I skipped away, in case it developed into a fracas.

How unfortunate. The dead president was a *Sardarji*. Dolly's impiety wounded the feelings of our cabby, who also happened to be a *Sardarji*. I could feel his anger rising. But he recovered his composure. His eyes were direct and searching, upon Dolly's face. He now sourly said:

'Never mind the hotel, *Memsaab*, please tell me where you want to go.'

'We don't know anyone here, *Sardarji*,' I told him politely.

'But you've got to have some place to go.'

'Oh, to hell!' The silly, headstrong girl, burst out savagely.

'Yes, *Memsaab*; but what about my petrol?'

'Your petrol?' Dolly gave him an angry look.

'Think, *Memsaab*, how far it is from here to hell.'

I almost laughed out aloud at this excellent ruse, but Dolly's look froze me.

'I'm sure you've enough petrol to reach us to Justice Puri's bungalow,' Dolly said, in a tone not to be denied.

'Certainly, *Memsaab*,' said the cabby, speeding the taxi into the night. After a long silence I heard the soliloquy – 'Justice Puri! The good man of the town.'

'So you know him?'

'Who doesn't?' To my half question, he answered, 'Every Chandigarhian knows him.'

'Is he a great man?'

'A man's man,' he said. And added: 'A very kind man.'

Disbelieving, I smiled at his boasting. That stung him. He shot a quick glance at me.

'That surprises you?'

'Yes, it does.'

'Why, you don't know him?'

'No. My wife knows him.'

Dolly gave him a cool smile and her direct look made him uncomfortable. After that, the poor fellow had to make a slight effort, to concentrate on his driving.

The taxi slowed down at the ring of the main road and I casually entered into conversation with Dolly.

'Now that sightseeing round places is over, I've to leave for Delhi tomorrow.'

'And I for my darling Bombay' Putting her neat nose in the air, she said with pride and delight, 'The great metropolitan city of love.' In next instant her excitement doubled just by the thought. 'Oh!' Simultaneously with her eyes shut and a soft exhalation of breath, she said, 'Oh, to be in Bombay!'

'Not breaking your journey at Delhi?'

'Nope.'

'I think the mytho-historical capital has all the attractions to hold a Bombay girl for a couple of days.'

'I salute the mytho-historical capital. As regards its attractions, I promise to taste them some other time.'

'Why not this time, since Delhi is on your way to Bombay?'

'Don't fret, my prince.' Grinning naughtily, she pinched the tip of my nose. 'Just drop a line and I shall come back to you. Promise.'

There came the end of our small talk when the taxi stopped in front of Justice Puri's bungalow. The driver looked at the meter and turned to me, mentioning the sum that I should pay. I gave him one fifty-rupee note, dismissing the change and Dolly, while alighting, favoured him with a wintry smile.

Twenty One

Justice Puri's Corinthian bungalow, painted lollipop-pink, standing out singularly in that lonely private sector, bespoke of the money expended in the service of taste. It stood majestic and alone, aloof and commanding, amid an acre of beautiful garden. Built in 1980 – the white, stone, cemented on the right pillar of the main gate proclaimed. The long driveway to the house, through the garden, had low hedges on both sides. A strong scent of jasmine in the air made me stand still, for a breather, before I entered the gate, which stood invitingly open.

Dolly had already moved in, slipping back one step for every two taken forwards and was waiting for me, near the closed door. As I stood beside her, a slight tremor passed through her frame.

'Don't you know him?' I asked, to clear my doubts.

'No,' she replied icily, keeping her eyes on the bell push.

Her cool 'no' first struck me with horror, then anger.

'What, you don't know him? Then how did you give Justice Puri's name?'

'If only you had used a little SS, you would have known.'

'SS? What on earth is that?'

'Gosh! You hulk of a man, you don't know what the two-letter code is?' Laughing at my ignorance, she enlightened me, 'SS stands for Sixth Sense.'

'Okay. But why Justice Puri? Why not Ghai-Rai, Sharma-Verma, Goel-Behl?'

'Because only certain names carry weight, not all. For example, Puri, Suri, Khosla, Khanna has always been a guarantee of quality, in the North. Among them I took an off-chance of quoting 'Puri', and it proved right.'

'But you cannot invite yourself into a stranger's household.'

'Why not, for heaven's sake? How else can one make friends otherwise?'

'Bright girl, we can be charged with attempted fraud, mind you!'

'May be I'm crazy, taking a chance like this.'

'Don't tell me I didn't warn you,' I said, shaking an admonitory finger at her.

'Leave the consequences to me. I'll take care of them.'

'What good is it, if you don't make use of your expensive education now?'

'Goddammit! I refuse to brush wits with you, anymore. I'm hungry. I don't wish to spoil my appetite.'

'But since when has hunger been a valid cause to perpetrate a crime?'

'For heaven's sake Sanchu, please stop it!'

Her hand moving challengingly towards the bell push, precipitated me into entreating.

'Don't, don't! Please, Dolly, don't!'

'Huh, who cares?' Now her hunger doubled with anger, she rudely pushed me aside. 'I'm hungry and absolutely refuse to starve for the sake of modesty.' And she jabbed her thumb on the bell push.

The harder I tried to pull her hand away, the ding-dong chorus of bells seemed to ring louder and louder.

She did everything she wanted to do in her own feminine, domineering way. Her nonsense had reached its zenith. No longer was it possible for me to withstand it. Feeling fearfully unsafe, as I turned to go, she stopped me, with a firm grip on my wrist.

'A true gentleman couldn't desert his companion at such a crucial moment.'

'Call me a scoundrel, I don't care. I can't put up with your obduracy anymore.' I wrenched my hand free.

'For better or for worse, you're staying here.' Leaping, she now grouted herself in front of me, obstructing my way.

'That may suit you, Miss Bohemian,' I said censoriously. 'It's not my style, to eat in somebody's house uninvited.'

This time, she was not getting anywhere with me. Fearing I may abandon her, she implored, with a melting smile.

'Sanchu, why don't you understand, this is not the time to argue, it's a time to act. And have no fears. You will have no scratches if you act as a sugar hubby.'

'Never! I don't want to play anyone's hubby.'

'Does it matter?'

'But I want you to play my hubby.'

'I don't share intimacies on command.'

'Just for tonight. Please...' she begged, with a choked voice.

'It's no use seducing me for something like that. I'm no actor.'

'Give it a try, please, for once.'

'No, I will not.'

'Pleeeeeease.'

'I will not.'

The closest I had come to losing my cool was when a creak of the door forced a stop, to our wordy duel. At once we both put on the 'Happily Married' smile, to win the heart of Mrs Puri.

As the door slowly opened, to our greatest surprise, the young man who had addressed us as 'Hello lucky pair' at the Yacht Club gate, stood staring at us.

I smiled at him and he smiled back, rather nervously.

'We would like to meet Mrs Puri,' said Dolly to him.

'Please come in,' he said, opening the door wider and stepping a side, to let us in.

Dolly looked relieved. 'It's hospitable of you to take us in.'

Our initial fear was gone and we walked in, with self-confidence.

Now the young man, with a guilty conscience, was trying to save his face. I guessed what was on his mind. He must have been thinking that we may report his behaviour to his mother. After a moment's hesitation he spoke in a shaky voice, 'Will you not be seated?'

We sat on the sofa he indicated. With lifted brows we were looking at his profile till, finally, he requested, 'Before I call mother, may I talk to you for a moment, please?'

'But I wanted to speak to your mother about something first.' Dolly was serious.

What will she say to his mother? The doubt and the fear, both were hammering at him, simultaneously. He assumed the worst, then thought of a way to deal with it.

'I never thought you would be offended. I'm really sorry for that.'

Dolly grinned. Extending a friendly hand, she said, 'Hey, it's settled.'

Gripping her soft hand, young Puri was all smiles. 'It's very good of you.'

Dolly, specialised in tricking and bluffing, was still holding the grip tight. She said, 'We need a favour from you.'

'Whatever you want, if I can help you,' was the spontaneous reply from Master Puri.

'No. I'm rather shy to ask you.'

'You need some cash? Don't you?'

'I'd never turn down that,' Dolly smiled, 'but it's something else.'

So far, so good, without voice, I shaped the words.

'Oh come on, whatever it is.' Master Puri looked very impatient.

'You really mustn't encourage me to impose on you.'

'Not at all. Don't be silly.'

'Well…'

'Well-well-well-well. I'm ready to do anything you want.'

'You know we're on our honeymoon. Our problem is… we aren't booked in any hotel and, we don't know anybody of this town. Under the circumstances, tell me, whom shall we turn to, for a place, until tomorrow morning?'

Master Puri was listening to Dolly in modest silence. But he couldn't hide his puzzlement, when, what was expected of him, was clear. He wasn't good at deception, nor had he any experience, like my companion.

Such an unusual request from a total stranger!

Dolly, reading his thoughts, said, 'I was hoping you could put us up for the night in a corner of your palatial bungalow… and, of course, you can say no and I'll understand.'

Moved by Dolly's magic words, Master Puri was now looking expansive. 'That's all you want?' He smiled a smile of understanding. 'You're my guests tonight,' laughingly assuring us, he retreated inside.

In the cosy drawing room, we did not have to wait long. Soon the curtain of the door was pulled aside and an aristocratic lady, superbly dressed and fortyish, appeared. The stares we got, were indescribable.

At once we rose to our feet composedly and our hands joined mechanically, in chaste '*namaste*'. But inwardly we felt jittery, now that she was actually here to meet two impostors.

She was like a *Ranee Saheba* of some erstwhile, Indian State, her head held high, as she came forward. I saw a flicker of surprise in her beautiful eyes. I avoided the glance, which was looking us over, discreetly judging, who we were and what our probable kinship with her, was. I felt as if my feet were sinking into quicksand. That was the moment my loving wife exclaimed:

'Sweetie Aunty!'

A strange girl, calling her by this name, surprised Mrs Puri. Yet there seemed to be a strong emotional tie between Mrs Puri and the name 'Sweetie Aunty'. Perhaps that was the reason why, in the next moment, she came forward with open arms to receive Dolly who rushed to fall upon the motherly bosom.

Dolly's wonderful performance and ready wit, gave me the utmost mental relief and I felt that a crisis had just passed.

Mrs. Puri poured out motherly affection on Dolly: 'My Anita! My dearest Anita!'

'No, Aunty, she is Dolly.' Automatically truth blasted out.

Dolly glared at me and I just shrank over my mistake.

'Yes, young man, your Dolly is my Anita.'

Narrowly saved, Dolly smiled her natural smile that had never failed to spread confidence, but her eyes had the admonishing look of a protective wife.

Sorry and uneasy, I looked away, only to find that Mrs Puri's careful eyes held on me, as though taking a mental x-ray.

Had she figured out what passed between us... Perhaps she wasn't as knowing as I imagined.

'Be seated, young man,' she said, waving a tapering, well-kept hand, adorned with ruby and diamond rings.

'Thank you, Aunty.' Sitting back on the sofa, unasked, I gave my name in order to gain her confidence, 'My name is Sanchu.'

'In short, in full it is Sanchayan,' Dolly explained.

'A fine name,' said Mrs Puri, with an understanding nod.

'A trusting name,' added Dolly grandly. 'Loveable, dependable, amiable, three-in-one.'

And as Dolly took pride in glorifying my name, I wore a happy face, to hide my embarrassment.

Though fairly impressed, Mrs Puri suppressed a smile – gave us a fact-finding look which I interpreted as *'I really like you two; you've got a totally different style'.* Aloud she said, 'Now tell me what you liked best of Chandigarh.'

'Of all, I liked the magnificent Assembly Hall the best. But the soul of Chandigarh is Nek Chand's Rock Garden – a wondrous, enchanting, wacky, mind-blowing creation. How rightly, some years ago, a French museum curator had written in the visitor's book: God has a competitor – Nek Chand.'

Mrs Puri smiled at the admiration but her shrewd, twinkling eyes were watching us intently and it seemed to miss nothing.

'Sukhna Lake, if you ask me, Aunty,' Dolly, quickly taking over, marched forward on the road to safety. 'Though it is a man-made one, it is superbly located; its varied scenery, Shivalik Hills, lakes and forests, the three together seem to be the harmonious blending of a united whole where the wind really blows free, where the vault of the sky seems smaller and the stars look more brilliant than anywhere else.'

'And where the people have time for friendship,' I lobbed the topic, from land, to people.

'And you know, Aunty, we don't know anybody here.'

'The trouble with her, is she can't go to bed hungry,' I pleaded for Dolly.

'You'd better stop spinning that yarn – I'm not a child.' Dolly gave me a murderous look, which I ignored.

'And your Chandigarh hoteliers are mourning the death of their Association President.'

'So?'

'A town-wide, general shutdown of hotels and restaurants.'

'And for that, you two, were on the lookout for an Aunty!'

There was a pregnant pause of one, silent minute. Fear gripped us, as the clock on the wall ticked.

Dolly's scheme, as it appeared to me, had almost come to a bad end. Danger signals began clanging in my brain. In that state of despondency, I tried not to notice the hard stares of Mrs Puri. I prayed, 'God help us now if ever you're going to help us'. While Dolly, thoroughly upset and shaken, jabbered fast, 'Yes aunty, no aunty.'

All this time, we kept talking irrelevantly, to confuse Mrs Puri but she was not the one to be confused by flippancy.

'Now leave this 'yes aunty, no aunty'. This is our dinner time. You're welcome.'

At once Dolly felt both soiled and reprimanded and turned to me, for guidance.

As nothing was left to guide or suggest, I looked up at the wall-clock, opting out of her schoolgirl scheme.

The time was then five minutes to eight.

Just below the wall-clock, hung the most popular colour picture (A photograph, not a living study) of the Father of the Nation and his great disciple, Nehru, both sharing a joke.

My eyes glued on it, my ears filled with the ripples of their hearty laughter, which was now surprisingly vibrant, in all reality.

Dolly, heaving audibly at my neutrality, looked within herself for strength and dignity. 'Well, Aunty...' she cleared her throat awkwardly, then proceeded, 'if it's not too much trouble...'

'Not another word! Come this way, our dinner time is promptly at eight,' came the affectionate command from the kind lady, inspite of everything. Dolly hid her feelings behind a calm, exterior and followed her, down the corridor to the dinning room. At the door, she stopped for a moment, looking back she thumbed her nose and wiggling her finger at me, she disappeared.

It was perhaps the crowning thrill of my prayer that had helped change the mind of our hostess, in a moment. In gratitude, I knelt down and thanked God. Then jumping to my feet, doubled up towards the door where I had seen Dolly disappear.

Twenty Two

So, at eight o'clock at night, with my pride in my pocket, I was sitting with the Puri family, in their elegantly furnished dining room. I wasn't hungry, but there's nothing like a meal to help a stranger grow acquainted.

It was not, of course, an ordinary meal. Rather, it was a gorgeous dinner, in a cosy atmosphere. A variety of subtly spiced dishes, arrayed in all finery, met my surprised gaze.

My acting wife, trained as she was to adaptability, was in fine fettle. Hungrily eyeing the mouth-watering dishes for some moments, she took a deep sniff, gave a hoop of joy, then said, gulping:

'Umm! Everything looks extremely delicious!'

'Really? You can't be sure.' Promptly, the host commented on Dolly's childish outburst.

'I'm doubly sure,' was Dolly's instant repartee.

'But you haven't tasted anything yet.'

'It's not necessary, Uncle.'

'If not, then how can you be that certain?'

'Basing an AT'

'AT! Never heard of it.'

'How can such a simple thing not be heard? Sheer lack of general knowledge. Very disappointing.'

A short, embarrassed silence, followed this profound statement. A little mortified by her precocity, I looked at her sternly. But her innocent face was devoid of any sarcasm. Luckily, our host possessed a robust sense of humour.

'So what? Educate me. One is never too old to learn.'

Now, filled with proven superiority, the chatty girl said wisely, 'A is for Aroma and T for Therapy.'

'You mean Aromatherapy shortened to AT?' asked our bewildered host.

'Yes, sir. And, it is this AT that says we eat food by sniffing first, then with, tongue.'

Maintaining an unassailable dignity until now, Mrs Puri enjoying this host-guest dinner talk, suddenly broke in. 'She's right. Absolutely right!' In addition, she quoted an age-old Sanskrit proverb, *Ghraaneno ardha-bhojanam* and winked at her husband, as one conspirator to another.

'It seems she is very good at Aromatherapy.' Mr Puri winked back.

'There's no question about it,' concurred Mrs Puri.

Then, the host and hostess glanced furtively at each other and smiled secretly.

But somehow, Dolly had discovered their little conspiracy. She preened defensively, protesting, 'I'll prove it to you, right here and now.' She ripped a piece of *tandoori roti*, dipped into the *dum aloo*, ate it and declared: 'See? I was right. It is delicious.'

Her childish delight brought out happy smiles off Mister and Missus Puri.

It was the flawless acting, which convinced them, that we were a happily married couple in real life.

For over ten minutes I had been sitting there, dumb. When hilarity was at the peak between childishness and tenderness, a western joke surfaced in my mind. Lured by the strategic, good timing, I was about to crack it. Dolly, as if reading my thoughts, whispered audibly in the host's ear, 'Uncle, Sanchu is very good at dinner jokes.'

'Really?' They exchanged a diabolic grin. Then, turning to me, Mr Puri said, 'Young man, we like dinner jokes.'

Encouraged by him, I looked at the others. All smiled and nodded. In deference to the collective wishes of the Puri family, I began:

'It is said, half the population of Europe believe that people in England live like kings and eat like pigs. In Hungary, they live like pigs and eat like kings. But...'

'The Chandigarhians live like *Rajahs* and eat like *Maharajahs*,' an overjoyed Dolly summed up. Then, to spice it further, she declared, 'And no better dinner has been served this night, in the whole of Chandigarh.'

In the wink of a whim, the oddity of her behaviour changed the course of the joke from western to Indian, that evoked a pleasant laughter.

Neither shocked nor appalled by this interference, I was pleased with her sense of humour.

'Two rogues!' Mrs Puri remarked with a smile.

'Let the English and Hungarians eat as they like,' said Mr Puri. 'Why do we not dine and wine like…' he stopped the question on his lips, while his eyes went from Dolly to me, and back to Dolly again.

Dolly, the brilliant conversationalist, taking up the hint, exclaimed, 'Like the *Maharajah* of Patiala!'

Once again there were ripples of mirth.

Soon after, the ripples of mirth settled to the soft tinkles of silver, against china.

A full, fifteen minutes elapsed, tinklingly.

At times Dolly, though childish, had always considered herself the only beauty on earth, not to have any request denied.

'I hope, Aunty will not mind our stay here, tonight.'

I smiled at the neat way she initiated this fresh conversation.

'This is your home, child. Your bed is ready on the ground floor, the first room on your right,' was the genial reply from Mrs Puri.

Dolly blushed, like a newly married girl.

'A word more. We're all heavy sleepers and if you happen to go early in the morning, please don't forget to leave your address on the writing-table.'

'Shhh,' cautioned Dolly, 'if he hears you asking for my address, he may also ask for it.'

'Whaat!' Justice Puri rapped out in awe.

'Yes, Uncle, I haven't given him my address yet.'

'That's not surprising, my child, for his address is now yours.'

Mrs Puri's maternal instinct sprang to Dolly's defence.

But Mr Puri's cool stare, mitigated by a smile, quickened my pulse beats.

During the rest of the dinner, Dolly monopolised the conversation, chattering on, in her inconsequential way and saying nothing of any real importance.

A thought crossed my mind that Dolly was the most unnatural girl in the world.

Twenty Three

After a long, lazy and lavish dinner, young Puri led us up to the door of the guest room.

'Make yourselves at home. I trust you'll find the double-bed cosy.' He gave me a naughty look and I winked at him.

'Goodnight,' said Dolly, smiling sweetly.

'Goodnight, lucky pair, a good, good night,' and he strode off, without a backward glance.

In the dimly lighted guest room, we paused, looking bashfully at each other. Silence weighed us down, as the implications flashed through our minds. That was when we realised that we were in a bottomless pit.

After making a photographic survey of the room, Dolly stood calm, pressing her back against the closed door. The room, dominated by an enormous double bed, with a snow-white cover on it, was not at all unpleasant. Rather, it was warm and suggested love and sweet sleep. The walls were painted sky-blue. There was a dresser and a writing table and a door, that led to a small bedroom. There was a built-in closet, with wire hangers in it and three windows,, with frilled, white curtains.

'I wish…'

'What?'

'I wish it wasn't the first thing you saw,' she said staring at the bed.

'But it's the bed that gives the name of the room, 'bedroom'.'

'I feel very guilty. Do you?'

'No.'

Dolly was not pleased with my negative answer. She said, 'You don't have to be so blunt.'

'I'm not blunt. I'm honest.'

'Are you blaming me completely for this?'

'Of course.'

'Go to hell.'

'I'm already there.'

She did see how dangerous the present situation was. So, when an angry retort came to her lips, but somehow, she managed to control it.

'Had it ever occurred to you, Dolly,' I begged her to understand, 'if the fraudulent intent of the married couple act, that we've so far successfully played, is uncovered, we can be sent behind bars?'

After that, some time passed in silence. This silence gave her time to think. She hadn't finished thinking; she was pacing the room reminding me of a caged tigress.

'Oh, I am so ashamed.' I heard her repenting at last. 'I'll never be able to forgive myself.'

'May be we can still leave,' I suggested.

'Can we?'

'Sure, we can,' was my confident assurance.

After careful consideration she said, 'No, it's a little too late,' and scurried to the double bed, refusing to act on my suggestion. Running a caressing hand over the bed, as if it were made of eggshells, she whispered loudly, 'What's better than a warm bed to a newly married couple, Sanchu?'

Though there was no nuance of passion in the utterance, I couldn't believe my ears. I countered, somewhat flippantly, 'How could I know? I'm merely an acting husband.'

'You're very smart, aren't you?'

'Listen Dolly, we're here, we're in it together, it's done.'

'That means you want to share this bed!'

'Why not? I'm your husband.' The words were out of my mouth like a shot from a bow.

'Nonsense. If a double bed is the ultimate goal of marriage, I'm not going to marry at all.'

'People who say such things are the first to get married.'

'Huh!' Her chin went up with pride and defiance. 'I will never be the chattel of some man. I will never be an unpaid servant, working eighteen hours a day for some male tyrant. Males earn bread and little women cook it; that is now a thing of the past.'

'My God! If all women begin to think like you, then extinction of the social and spiritual bond between man and woman is not far off.'

'Nothing matters. Women can get along without men. The woman of today sits on brain's trusts and committees, run things and governs countries, unlike her Victorian predecessor, whose relaxation was tittle-tattle. Therefore, there's no need for woman of today to seek this legalised protection.'

In truth, Dolly did not know about the complex tangle of loyalties and obligations that constituted a marriage. In reply to her outrageous opinion, I simply said:

'Marriage is designed primarily for giving, rather than taking. It is meant to be a permanent union of two, unselfish people.'

'If marriage is meant to be a permanent union, why do people get divorced? Have you any answer to this? Obviously no. I, therefore, consider your philosophical view about marriage as sham and hypocritical.'

'From the way you put it, I gather you're dead against marriage.'

'Though the divorce rate in our country is alarmingly on the rise, still I'm a firm believer in mankind's oldest institution - marriage. I think it is beautiful, wonderful and admirable. But I'm dead against a marriage that licences husbands to run wives. What a woman wants most, is an understanding partner, who shares her concerns rather than the chauvinist, who uses his wife as an emotional prop and expects his concerns to be paramount.'

'No sane person would deny a rightful status to his wife. The Hindu scriptures describe home as *Grihini grihamuchyate*, i.e. the wife is the heart of the home. The venerable *Manu*, ancient Hindu lawgiver, ordains: Where the women are honoured, there the gods dwell. Can there be a higher, or loftier conception of woman, than this?'

'*Grihini grihamuchyate* - how ridiculous that phrase sounds when, in practice, all your rightful status, higher and loftier conceptions are systematically denied once the ceremony is over. The husband becomes the sole master of his wife. What greater or better deceit can there be, than this?'

'That's a terrible accusation.'

'No. It's not an accusation. It is fact based on day-to-day happenings. Husbands, for centuries, have been suppressing wives, deceiving and exploiting them, on some pretext or the other. Not to mention the unforgiving brutalities.'

'But you're overlooking the fact that wise men have always given women their dreams.'

'Men are dream merchants. They often try to sell imaginary ideas to their wives, for sex. Fortunately, today women are more practical. They know how to deal with them if they are not in a mood, or not keeping well.'

To keep the argument in view I twisted it a bit. 'What is really noteworthy is that women are delicate creatures. From the beginning of civilisation, they welcomed marriage for security and comfort.'

'Women, being anatomically smaller than men, are physically weaker. They welcomed marriage because of environment and training. But, luckily, they don't have smaller brains than men.'

'Women might have brains that are equal to men's brains. But being biologically a different species, mentally and physically, their spheres are different from a man's sphere and their truths are often contradictory. The reality is, that men and women are utterly different creatures and their biological difference is the major gap, that prevents them, from being men's equal.'

'Don't be so gender biased. Today's women are more self-assured. They are the contenders in every field.'

'That's why, to make it easy for women to get through, a majority of chauvinistic politicians have introduced the Women's Reservation Bill, allowing concessions and granting relaxations.'

'These are political tricks of the pretenders, I mean politicians, to gain support and win votes. Women don't need any kind of concession, relaxation or reservation, except those calling for great physical strength to prove their enormous talent and power as professional people.'

'So you see, you admit man's innate superiority. But actually, men don't just think they are superior; they have been the boss, by virtue of size and strength, for so long, that the 'feel' of superiority has become ingrained. Yet, in fairness to the wives, gradually, husbands give them a fifty per cent partnership.'

'Rubbish!' Dolly was now red in the face. 'Wives don't need husbands' fake fifty per cent partnership.'

'There's no sense in losing your temper. A Hindu home is structured on those genial facts of life.'

'Change your style of thinking, man.' Dolly ridiculed. 'Those are not facts of life but a few of the many unquestioned privileges men have been enjoying for ages. Our laws need revising. A husband should not have so many rights over his wife. It damages a woman's dignity. The hallowed tradition of '*Pati Parameshwar*' is outdated.'

'The Hindu tradition is built on discharging one's duties rather than insisting on one's rights over the other. One is not a slave, even to traditions, for the Hindu wife *finds* her partner in life.'

But all my attempts to steer her to our heritage were rudely rebuffed.

'For god's sake, stop being preachy. I've had enough of your *Upanishadic* wisdom. No use sermonising me on Hindu culture.'

'Avoiding the issue doesn't mean it does not exist. It exists.'

'Even if I'm not a believer of your doctrinal principles?'

'Nothing doctrinal. It's the plain truth.'

'I don't want to fight with you, Sanchu. Only don't foist those doctrines on me. Don't try to make me see things your way, because I can't.'

Momentarily, I was flummoxed and didn't know what to say. But Dolly seemed to have a lot more to say. Her sullen face and gathered brows clearly indicated that she was nursing her wrath, to keep it warm.

'Forgive me, Dolly,' I began smoothly, 'it is distressing to know that you're so much against marriage.'

'Yes, I am and I always shall be.'

'You never know what the future has, in store for you.'

'I already know.'

'Do you?'

'Yes,' she said, adding 'if the present marriage conditions are not changed, I would prefer to remain a spinster all my life. Quite frankly, I don't need a man to rule my life.'

'God! That's too much'

'I suppose I've surprised you by saying such a thing.'

'Surprised? Surely I am. If every girl thinks like you, then, perhaps boys will either remain bachelors to the end of their days or turn into hermits.' A short, half-amused laugh that I couldn't control, irritated her.

'It's all right for you to laugh, Sanchu, now that I'm trapped within these four walls.'

The word 'trapped' touched my self-respect and I lost my temper.

'You asked for trouble. Or did I?'

'You can lord your will on me, if you want to.'

'Don't let that bother you, Dolly. I shan't corrupt you.'

'You saint!' She pounced upon me like an enraged tigress, grabbed my shirt and shook me. 'Don't you dare think of corrupting me.'

'Won't you be quiet, Miss Purity? Or do you want to land me into further trouble?' I asked, in a conciliatory tone, which only maddened her further.

'So, I've landed you into trouble, you smooth-talking rascal!' Dolly's voice rose several decibels more. 'Get the hell out of here. I don't want to see you another moment.'

'I'm immune to the abuse you think fit, to heap on me, Miss Dolly,' I said tolerantly, keeping my grave eyes on her. 'Surely, hard words break no bones, but I must beg you to remember, that Mrs Puri is in the next room.'

As I took the name of our kind hostess, the door flew open and in came Mrs Puri.

All at once, the never-to-be-ended argument, stopped.

'What's going on?' inquired Mrs Puri after an instant survey. Her voice was sub zero.

'Oh, nothing Aunty, just enjoying each other's company,' I lied and made a valiant effort to smile.

'I think you two are awfully rough with each other.'

'Insults don't bother me anymore. I have had them with breakfast, lunch and dinner, ever since we're married.'

'Don't quarrel so much. The more you quarrel, the more you weaken the nuptial knot and a day may come soon, when it will not have the strength to hold you together.'

'That's what I was trying to explain to him, Aunty; only he must understand…' and she started crying.

The ready bluff and crocodile tears blurred the absolute truth and convinced Mrs Puri that her Anita was telling no lie.

'My child, in this male-dominated world, women are the worst sufferers of discrimination,' Mrs Puri began comforting her by focussing on the faults of male domination. 'Indian women, they are the primarily underdogs of an exploitative society, unsafe on the streets and sexually harassed, at work. At home, they are often worse off, reduced to slavish drudges, constantly derided, frequently bullied, sometimes assaulted and occasionally burnt to death. They are maltreated in a hundred different ways and they have suffered this, meekly and quietly.

'Now at last, from every corner of the country, our women have began to stir: the protests over rape, the angry *morchas* against *dowry,* the rising clamour for equality in jobs, in law, in education, in status. All this spell one thing – a time for reckoning.' Suddenly, Mrs Puri paused to check the effect of her oratory on me.

After this barrage of criticism, a hot protest trembled on my lips. But I restrained myself. I wondered what made this fine lady, who had charmed me earlier by her elegance and sophistication, pour out this stream of indignation. Every word she said was directed at me, as I was the only male present there, then, as if every male is an object of hatred.

Equally suddenly, in a lighter vein, she concluded, 'However, we women are not chauvinistic. We regard ourselves as that part of human race, which is facing a great crisis. Society should not be biased in favour of either the male, or the female. I think a combination of the talents of both the sexes would bring in better uniformity. With this in mind, we women, as a parallel civilising force, desire to create a New World, along with our menfolk.'

But no, she didn't conclude it there. Before I could breathe a sigh of relief, I heard her say the worst.

'Remember, Anita, for one moment of surrender you're to live through a thousand moments of shock and suspense.'

Hurt by Mrs Puri's unjustified dictum, as I was about to open my mouth in protest, she silenced me with a frosty stare. Then, with totally unexpected bonhomie, she said:

'Now it's bedtime. You two are old enough to be left alone in a bedroom to do things other than quarrel.' With these final words she chugged out, slamming the door hard.

Stupefied, I turned my gaze on my companion who, blushing a beetroot red, hid her face in her palm. But the moment our hostess was out of the room, she was convulsed with giggly laughter.

'Stop giggling!' I commanded roughly.

That made her hysterical.

'So far I've tolerated your bohemian ways but I can't stomach it anymore.'

'Really?' She mocked, forcing the word through her giggle.

'Stop or I'll make you cry.'

It was an empty threat I would never carry out, but it stopped her convent giggle.

Struck dumb, she was now gaping at me, like sheep in the stare of a python.

'Don't compel me to expose you. Once I do, expect no mercy.'

This time, I probably didn't sound convincing and it altered the outcome.

'Damn your mercy.' Waving the threat away as casually as she might have brushed a fly from her nose, she challenged, 'How far can you get away from it, is the question. No doubt it's a silly game, but we both are playing it. If you think by telling Aunty you will be safe, please do so, by all means…'

The shrewdness of Dolly left me speechless.

'Huh, threatening me?' She gave me a severe look, and then kicking off her shoes, she jumped into bed. With her head pressed to the pillow and her back turned to me, she started to undo the buttons of her blouse.

Long afterwards, the sound of yawning made itself heard in the silence. Still pleased with her make-believe, Dolly put her hand to her mouth, to hide another elaborate yawn.

'Oh, I'm so sleepy,' she muttered to herself. Then, with her characteristic changeability, she asked sweetly, to the pleasure of her adopted husband, 'Aren't you coming, Sanchu darling?'

'You mean I should sleep with you?'

'Yes, of course. Here, with me,' slapping the bed, she cajoled me. With much difficulty she curbed her giggle and hurried on raising her voice so that Mrs Puri could hear, in the next room. 'After all, we're husband and wife. The sensible citizens of this town have already turned off their lights and gone to bed.' Yawning tiredly, she switched off the bedside lamp. 'Goodnight, sweet prince,' she whispered, slipping towards sleep.

'Goodnight, sweetheart,' I said aloud, to keep up the deception.

In the darkness, the room felt suddenly stuffy. Softly moving to the window, I looked out at the starry sky.

The battle over marriage and rights, however, rested for the night without restoring our former concord. It was the longest night of my life, which I spent sitting near the window, counting stars, while her Royal Highness slept soundly, with a trusting smile on her lips.

The dawn, like all dawns, broke beautifully. As the grey haze began to spread, I woke her up. First she stirred, then yawning, opened her drowsy eyes and smiled that marvellously infectious smile, that could light a room and sweep everything along with it. But I ignored her, with calm indifference.

For the first time the 'boomerang' missed its target.

Sitting on the edge of the bed, she was watching me in silence perhaps for half a minute, then, rising, she crossed the room to the mirror. While brushing her hair, a contrite Dolly spoke to the reflection, that rebounded to me.

'Now I realise how horribly I had behaved last night.'

'Past history. No use thinking about it now.'

'No, it's not past. It's very much present.'

'Please don't pester me, early in the morning. There isn't much sense brooding over it.'

'Won't you forgive me?'

'Honestly speaking, I'm grateful to you.'

I haven't done anything like that. Actually, I piled many hard words on you.'

'Don't bother, it's all over now. Get ready fast. It's about time we left this place.'

Poor Dolly, failing to draw me into a compromise, turned to the mirror, with a broken heart, to give final touches to her angel face.

Meanwhile, I wrote a note of thanks:

Dear Aunty,

By the time you read this note, we'll be far away. But your hospitality will remain with us forever. Please forgive us leaving like this. Thanks for everything.

Your loving rogues,

Dolly & Sanchu.

Leaving the thank you note on the writing table, we tiptoed out the bedroom door, shoes in hand and did not put it on, until we passed through the main gate and onto the street. A sharp final clink, not very loud, of wrought iron, relieved me from the pangs of worries. I stood for a moment with the guilty air of a burglar and turned imperceptibly, for a hurried glance at the house.

The house was still and peaceful.

Unutterably sad, I took a deep breath and asked Dolly, 'Don't you feel bad, to leave like this.'

'Needn't feel bad. Think about the jolly, good time we gave them, just for a dinner.' Whether out of ignorance or arrogance, God knows, she continued to emphasise her point. 'Hosting a honeymooning couple is a rare privilege and could have gone to someone else, had I so desired. The Puri family will remember us for years to come.'

Up to the last word, I listened patiently, hiding what I felt deep within me and arrived at this conclusion: 'Perhaps she wasn't human. If she were, she wouldn't make such remarks in that callous cold-blooded way!'

'It's not the time to stand and stare,' she said impatiently, breaking into my thoughts. 'Come, let's go. No time to waste.' Linking her arm through mine, she practically frog-marched me, to the main road and yelled at a passing taxi.

Twenty Four

At the station, we had coffee and sandwiches and by the time we reached the platform, the Mail was awaiting the green signal.

Sitting in the train, Dolly smiled at me. Looking deep into my eyes, she held my hand, warm and friendly.

We lingered like that, rather long, touched by melancholy. Perhaps, both of us, for the first time, had realised that the joyous journey was fast coming to an end.

In time, the signal turned green, the whistle blew, the engine tooted, the train jerked and slowly chugged out of the platform, into the morning sun. The houses began to tread on each others heels; a hotel was followed by a restaurant, a *temple* by a *gurudwara*, finely illustrated advertisements of sports goods and auto spares swarmed closer together. When at last the public buildings were squeezed out, changing urban scenery into pleasing, rural greenery, I opened the conversation:

'Care to spend a day or two in the capital?'

'You've asked that before, haven't you?'

'Well yes. I have.'

'Then why do you ask again?'

'Thought you might have changed your mind.'

'Not a chance. My mind has already reached Bombay.'

'Oh…' That was all I could find, to say, so chilling was Dolly's reply. Emotionally drained, I kept looking at her, silently.

Dolly, completely detached, was now looking out of the window. All of a sudden, her great interest in the swift, changing scenery, iced the remnants of the warm feelings that were left within me.

For what seemed a very long time, we did not say anything.

It was she who spoke first, 'I didn't mean to hurt you Sanchu,' her voice quite, genial. 'Don't think otherwise; may be another time, another place.'

'How? When? Where?'

'How can I say? Only the future can tell.'

'Certainly you can tell, unless you want to break away.'

She said nothing, only sighed softly. But there was something in her eyes, some deep, ruffled expression, that puzzled me.

The train had gained speed now and was heading for Ambala, leaving behind India's prestigious, planned town, Chandigarh. Keeping my eyes on the passing scenery, I remained silent. The soft breeze, feathering through Dolly's hair, stilled into breathless silence. A strand of her hair blew across my lips; I smiled, uncertainly this time and she tightened one arm about me.

'Meeting you; getting history lessons; touring historical places with you... I shall never forget them. It has been one of the most beautiful times of my life.'

'Hey, you make it sound as if you are saying goodbye.'

'Why do you think so, Sanchu? There's every chance of our meeting again. Somewhere, someday soon.'

'Sure. Why not? After all, meeting and parting is the cycle of life.'

'And always there is a tomorrow.'

'Huh, tomorrow!'

When Dolly saw my pained expression, she riposted, 'Yes, there will be a tomorrow for both of us and life for us, will begin anew.'

'You're wrong to be so confident in the existence of tomorrow.'

The truth in my statement brought a look of sudden pensiveness to her eyes. Then her words broke through her tears.

'Didn't we agree we would be parting at Delhi? It was a gentleman's agreement. Remember?'

'But why does it have to be just that?'

Taking a deep breath, she said, 'It would be a sweet world, Sanchu, if all the things went on as we wished.'

'Is this, then, the end?'

'No. Our friendship is forever. It is based on understanding and respect. It has a beginning. It has no end.'

'Will our friendship never change into love?'

'I don't think anyone can change, if we're destined to be close friends and never lovers.'

'I can change.'

Dolly was outwardly surprised and inwardly pleased.

'Are you certain? Or is it just an empty boast?'

'I am certain, only if you agree to be my guest at Delhi, to prove how right I am.'

She looked at me for a long moment and then shook her head. 'That's not possible.'

'Then let's make a promise.'

'Oh, sure,' she answered at once.

We both knew what promise we wanted to make and with infinite pleasure, almost univocally, we mouthed the words 'FOREVER YOURS'. We said no more and in affirmation, we shut our eyes, holding each other tight and feeling the friendship.

Mixed with adoration and happiness, Dolly was near tears. Quickly, she turned her face, so that I may not see the sudden wetness of her eyes.

After some moments of silence, her eyes met mine. I could see in her wet eyes, the still waters of the Khadakwasla Lake, the blooming lotuses of the Munj Talao, the lurching yacht on the crystal waters of the Sukhna Lake. Suddenly, the still water of the three lakes turned into violent waves, shook down the petals of the lotuses and sank the lurching yacht. I got lost in those dark, beautiful eyes and time slipped away...

Suddenly, noticing a narrow river of tears gleaming on her face as I laid my hand on hers, she said, 'I'll ever be indebted, Sanchu.'

'You owe me nothing, my dearest. On the contrary, I'm glad to be of service.'

A sad smile flickered across her face.

'Just because the journey is going to end doesn't mean we have to let our friendship go to the dogs. If anything, we must renew our pledge 'Forever Yours,' I reasserted.'

After that, there fell another golden silence between us, that made Dolly draw nearer me, without realising that she did so.

Deliberately, slowly, she clutched me in such a complete intimate embrace, that I could feel the pressure of her thighs and the softness of her breasts. There, the way she was, she would have yielded to me, in whatever way, I wanted. This was clearly the moment. Too big. Too full. Too ripe.

In that unguarded moment, shyness had steadily crept in and, colouring a little, she turned her face away. Looking out, she waved a hand, to indicate the green countryside through which the train was passing. The clickety-clack of wheels on track, the rasp and jerk of couplings, as bogies rounded a sharp bend, made my heart beat faster.

Then, soon, too soon, drowsiness came over me, driving me to doze on Dolly's shoulder. Probably, the previous sleepless night had silently begun to affect me, before I knew what was happening.

Tenderly cradling me, she pressed my head on her bosom. The warmth of her bosom under my cheek, felt like the ultimate comfort, in the whole world. I snuggled in a trance of relief and gratitude, while she patted my cheek.

'Sleep, Sanchu, you didn't sleep a wink last night.'

My sleeplessness and her supple nearness, wooed me into a perfect sleep. Within seconds, I had passed beyond the reach of dreams, accompanied by the rhythm of the wheels.

Twenty Five

When no nearness was too close, when no word needed to be spoken, the train had entered that typical, enclosing sound of a railway station. As it slowly came to a halt, I stirred and rubbed my eyes. It must be Delhi, I thought to myself. Sitting up, I turned to look at Dolly. But Dolly wasn't there. Assuming she would be in the toilet, I waited. Even when two anxious minutes had lapsed and she didn't turn up, I went towards the toilet door and stood there, listening for the sounds of running water but none was coming from within. Letting a few seconds pass, I flung open the door.

No Dolly; no one was there. But a message 'Dolly Loves Sanchu' was pencilled with lipstick, on the toilet mirror.

What a novel way to say goodbye! The thought crossed my mind, but I dismissed it. Back to my seat when I found that her things, too, had disappeared along with her, a pain of desertion began to swell within me and in trying to resist, it burst with hysterical relief.

I did not want to doubt her love and did not doubt it, but the hammering of a single question: *Why should she suddenly disappear?* - kept torturing me.

Had I given her cause to distrust me? Fear me? Surely I hadn't. Then what was the reason? Whatever the reason, she shouldn't have played the vanishing trick. Had she told me she was leaving, I wouldn't have held her back, by force.

Racing over every possible answer to the grim question, I concluded: *No use thinking about her anymore. She has gone, never to return.* Tears welled up in my eyes.

'If you have any sense of responsibility, you should inform the police,' the psychological fear inside me focussed, despite the fact that she was quite capable of taking care of her worldly self.

I knew nothing about her, except what she had told me. Her background could have been fictitious; she could have made it all up.

Now, with only the first name, Dolly, how was I going to see the police? It was then and only then, that I became aware of a grave omission: that at no time had she given me any indication of her identity, except her first name, nor had it occurred to me to ask her. We were so happy in each other's company that the thought did not seem of any importance then.

Heaving a sigh over my lack of common sense, I pushed the thought away and resolved to make not the least resistance to fate, no matter in what form it presented itself to me.

Somehow, mastering my mind, as I stepped out onto the crowded platform, I heard a voice that sounded like Dolly's calling me. For a timeless moment, I stopped dead still, while my eyes strained on all sides. Not finding her, I cried 'Dolly, where are you?' And then laughed at my sentimental absurdity; got into the crowd, taking with me the pleasant memory of ninety-nine hours of unspoken togetherness.

Glossary

Apsara	A heavenly nymph.
Badsahi bidi	Hand-rolled Indian cigar.
Bengali	A Bengali is a person from West-Bengal, a state in eastern India.
Bindi	The auspicious, vermilion dot mark noticeable on the forehead of Hindu, married woman.
Chaiwalla	Tea boy.
Chamchas	Talebearers
Didi	Affectionate term for an elder sister.
Draupadi	The name of the common wife of the five sons of Pandu – Mahabharata.
Dum Aloo	An aromatic Indian delicacy made with potatoes
Dupatta	An oblong silk or chiffon cloth, worn especially by women of northern India, as a covering for the head.
Fakir	A Hindu or Mohammedan ascetic beggar – a bona fide poor man.
Gajra	Flowers, woven into garlands, worn by women, to adorn braids of hair.
Haryanvi	A person from the Indian state of Haryana.
Heer Ranjha	The legendary lovers mentioned in a popular folk ballad, of the same name, from Punjab.
Jhoomkas	Ear rings.
Katchcha	Unmettled dirt track.
Maharajah	An Indian prince of higher degree than a rajah
Mahatma	A great soul.
Nathni	Nose ring.

Pamella Bordes	A Bombay girl, who was Miss India in 1982 and by 1989, she was the darling of London's high society. A House of Commons research clerk by day and a call-girl by night, her double life episodes rocked Westminster in the late eighties.
Pati Parameshwar	A husband is equal to God.
Pochas	Head dress, in the form of a garland worn by village women.
Prana	The life force.
Raaga	Any of a large number of traditional, melody patterns, used by Indian musicians.
Rajah	An Indian king.
Ranee Saheba	A reigning queen.
Rosogolla	The famous Indian sweet of Bengali origin.
Sarkanda	A species of tall grass.
Sardarji	
Sardar-Sahib	A Sikh
Sari	A five and a half metre cloth worn especially by Indian women, wrapped around the body in a laid down style.
Sati Savitri	The legendary, faithful wife who managed to get back alive her dead husband by pursuing Yama, the God of death.
Seeta	Lord Rama's wife who had to walk through fire, to prove her chastity – Ramayana.
Thaali	A metallic tray, much used in Indian hotels, for serving food.
Vivekanand	The great Hindu scholar.
Yaar	A friend.
Yudhishthira	The eldest of the Pandava brothers, who never lied – Mahabharata.